A DEADLY WEB

A DEADLY WEB

Jeanne M. Dams

SEVERN
HOUSE

First world edition published in Great Britain and the USA in 2022
by Severn House, an imprint of Canongate Books Ltd,
14 High Street, Edinburgh EH1 1TE.

Trade paperback edition first published in Great Britain and the USA in 2023
by Severn House, an imprint of Canongate Books Ltd.

severnhouse.com

British Library Cataloguing-in-Publication Data
A CIP catalogue record for this title is available from the British Library.

ISBN-13: 978-0-7278-5046-1 (cased)
ISBN-13: 978-1-4483-0779-1 (trade paper)
ISBN-13: 978-1-4483-0778-4 (e-book)

Typeset by Palimpsest Book Production Ltd.,
Falkirk, Stirlingshire, Scotland.

ONE

I was dozing in front of the fire while a storm raged outside. March in my adopted English home can be delightfully warm and sunny, with spring flowers abounding. It can also produce weather as nasty as weather can get, cold and grey, with that revolting precipitation that the weathermen back home in Indiana used to call 'wintry mix'. Rain, sleet, and snow, driven by furious winds, made my snug seventeenth-century house a blessed refuge. Add a large mutt asleep on the hearth rug, two cats sharing my squashy chair, and a bulky, comfortable husband nodding on the sofa, and not even the occasional crash of sleet thrown against the windows could keep me awake.

Alan's mobile pinged loudly. 'Drat!' he said as he struggled awake. 'Probably a telemarketer.' He pulled the phone out of his pocket, patted a couple of buttons, and then turned on the floor lamp beside him, the afternoon having darkened early in the dreadful weather. 'Now, who on earth . . . oh, I don't believe it. Lucy, of all people!'

I yawned and sat up a little straighter, disturbing Samantha, who indicated her displeasure with a full-throated Siamese yowl. 'Who's Lucy?'

'My great-niece. Well, not officially. Her grandmother, Jennifer, was Helen's dearest friend, so Helen and I became honorary aunt and uncle to Jennifer's daughter Susan, and the relationship passed on to Susan's girl, Lucy. Lucy . . . I can't remember her surname at the moment. I haven't seen her in years. Susan and her husband moved to Ashford when Lucy was seven or eight, so she went to school there, and then moved with her family to America when Lucy was eleven or twelve. Susan kept in touch for a while, but then she and her husband were killed in a plane crash. Lucy wrote to me when that happened, but that must have been seven or eight years ago. Since then there's been only a card or two marking milestones in her life.'

Helen was Alan's first wife, dead some years before I, newly widowed and newly moved to England, met him on a Christmas Eve in Sherebury Cathedral, our magnificent neighbour. A friendship rapidly developed into something more, and we'd been happily married for several years now. Alan retired from his position as chief constable of Belleshire, Sherebury's county, and we enjoyed a leisurely life punctuated now and then with involvement in other people's troubles.

'Poor child. I hope she had some family to fall back on.'

'I don't believe she did, actually. She was just about to enter university, and there was plenty of money – her father had been something important in electronics – so she simply carried on. Took a degree in finance, or business, or some such area, at the University of Indiana—'

'Indiana University,' I interrupted. 'Why there?'

'I don't know, but I believe they lived in Indianapolis. Is that nearby?'

'Relatively. Go on.'

'Well, then she went on to a doctorate in some related field at Chicago University – or is it the University of Chicago?'

'The latter. Confusing, I know.'

'At any rate, she tells me she now has a position having to do with fundraising at a small university near Chicago. And apparently she's quite good at her job, because she's coming to Sherebury at the end of April to head a conference on the subject at the university.'

'Ah! And that's why she texted you.'

'Indeed. She says she'll write a proper letter soon, but she wants to know when she might visit. Of course, love, I do realize you've never met the girl, and I barely know her myself, so do you think we're obliged to—'

'You're her beloved Uncle Alan. If she didn't want to see you again, she wouldn't have bothered to say she was coming. Of course we'll be happy to entertain her. Tell her she can stay with us if she likes. I'm sure there's nothing much on our calendar for late April. Easter's early this year, so we'll be free of church obligations. Text her right back and tell her she's most welcome. Or better yet, call her.'

Alan looked at his phone. 'Hmm. Almost six here. That'd be close to one in Chicago.'

'Noon, actually. Chicago's an hour earlier than Indiana.'

He chuckled. 'Good thing I have you to keep me up on matters American. I'll call.'

While he pulled out his phone and went through the somewhat complicated process of making an international phone call, I went to the kitchen. We'd forgotten to have tea, and I knew Alan would be starving, so I pulled a cottage pie out of the freezer and started it thawing in the microwave. I usually stick to very American food, as it's what I've cooked all my life, but I happen to love cottage pie, and it's easy.

It was just beginning to be fragrant, ready to go into the oven for a final browning, when Alan came into the kitchen. 'She sounds delighted at the idea of seeing both of us. Bubbly, actually. I'd forgotten how excited the young can get over even a minor treat. I'd hardly have thought she'd thrill to the idea of spending some time with two old fossils, one of whom she's never even met, but you'd have thought I was offering her the Christmas gift she'd always wanted.'

'What do you mean, fossils? Speak for yourself, Methuselah! But was she always a silly young thing?'

'Actually, I remember her as a rather quiet, serious-minded child. But of course she's been in America for years.'

I glared at the implied slur on my native land, and he grinned. 'A little nip of something, my dear?'

'If you think plying me with liquor will make me forgive you . . .'

'It usually does. Bourbon or wine?'

We settled amicably on wine with supper, with perhaps a wee dram of something later.

'You know,' I said as I put the steaming pie on the kitchen table, 'I wonder why a quiet, sensible child would turn into a flake. No offense, dear, but I doubt it's the possibility of seeing dear old Uncle Alan after all these years. Nor do I think it's the influence of the wild and woolly colonies. I'm placing my bet on an older and more potent influence.'

Alan frowned. 'You think she's on drugs?'

'The policeman's mind! No, I think she's in thrall to the

most powerful drug of all. She's in love. Here, hand me your plate.'

We argued the point as we ate our cottage pie and salad. 'I agree,' said Alan, 'that she sounded on the phone more like a lovesick teenager than a professional woman in her mid-twenties. But why would that make her delighted to see us?'

'It could be just the excitement of coming home again.'

'America's been her home for years. The formative years at that. Her accent and vocabulary are almost pure Yank. More salad?'

'No, thanks, but you might make some coffee. And pop the apple crumble in the oven while you're up.' Back home we called it apple crisp, and it's been one of my favourite desserts since I was a child. And I have to admit, the cream that goes over it is even better in this land than in Indiana.

We enjoyed our dessert and gave our demanding cats their expected treat of a little cream. Cream is not very good for cats. The house rule is, no begging at the table. Sam and Emmy, of course, ignore both strictures. Watson, our dog who also loves table scraps, is growing old and is no longer quite so alert when humans sit down to a meal. I set aside a little bit of the cottage pie for him, picking out the vegetables. He could have it later when he woke up.

After we'd cleared the table, Alan poured each of us a small tot of our preferred after-dinner drinks, bourbon for me, Scotch for him, and we settled back down in front of the fire.

'So, Sherlock, have you come up with any more ideas about Lucy's visit?'

Alan shrugged. 'Perhaps she's just excited about leading the conference. She's rather young for that sort of honour.'

'Nonsense! If it were at Oxford or Cambridge, now, I could understand. But she's got a Ph.D. from the University of Chicago, Alan! That's one of the prestige universities in America, in some fields right up there with the Ivy League.' I glanced at him.

He nodded to show he knew what the Ivy League was. 'I'm not quite an ignoramus, love.'

'No, but I never know how familiar you are with American

institutions. Anyway, for Lucy, Sherebury University is pretty small potatoes.'

'Then I am baffled, said Inspector Lestrade. This a mystery we shall never solve. I wonder if I might help myself to some of your cocaine, Mr Holmes?'

'I'm all out, but you can have another drop or two of whisky. And pour me a little more bourbon while you're at it. As for solving the mystery, I expect we'll figure it out once she gets here. Is there anything worth watching on the telly?'

Then Easter was nearly upon us, and living literally in the shadow of the Cathedral, we were caught up in Holy Week activities, the pomp and hosannas of Palm Sunday leading to the solemnity of Maundy Thursday and the grimness of Good Friday and finally to the radiant joy of Easter itself. I got out my favourite Easter bonnet, a Queen Mum affair covered in violets, and sailed off to church with Alan. I had loved all the Holy Week liturgies at home in my small church in Hillsburg, Indiana, and I loved them still in the great Cathedral. They were done with more elaborate ceremony here, and with incomparable music, but the amazing message was the same, and I was as always filled with awe and exultation.

I think it's a law of nature that the big highs in life are always followed by lows. It's true for me, anyway. I moped around the house on Easter Monday. There didn't seem to be anything to do. I'd cleaned thoroughly the week before, since we'd had guests for Easter dinner. There was so much in the way of leftovers that I wouldn't need to cook for days. The weather had remained surly, too wet to make walking Watson a pleasure; he'd been relegated to quick trips to the back garden when nature called. None of the mysteries on the bookshelf held any appeal. In short, I was bored and depressed and out of temper.

Fortunately Alan is used to my moods and amazingly tolerant of them. When I'm utterly impossible, he takes himself off to his study and works on the memoir he's been writing for years, and leaves me to stew in my own juice.

Finally, mid-week, I got sick of my own snit, found a hat,

and walked over to evensong at the Cathedral (the rain having finally abated). That lovely, peaceful service almost always snaps me out of whatever ails me. I came home to find Alan sitting surrounded by all three animals, with a glass in front of him, and one already poured for me.

'The sun isn't over the yardarm,' I commented.

'As you tell me Frank used to say, it must be five o'clock somewhere. Cheers. Glad to have you back.'

'I don't know why you put up with me,' I responded, taking a restorative sip of bourbon.

'Yes, you do. You're a marvellous cook and a pleasant companion. Most of the time.' He grinned and I, finally restored to my right mind, grinned back.

'And this marvellous cook is sick and tired of ham and various past-their-prime vegetables. Let's go out for dinner.'

'I've booked us in for six, at the Rose and Crown. A bit early, I know, but it won't be crowded then.'

'You read my mind. We've been married too long.'

'Not nearly long enough, my love. I have mentioned from time to time, have I not, that you're transparent?'

'And must never play poker. Right. And I may have mentioned that I adore you. Or maybe not, seeing as how that would embarrass your English sensibilities. I hold you in great and respectful esteem.'

'I'll drink to that. Now drink up, and go put on your Sunday best, as you word it. I'm treating my best girl to dinner!'

TWO

The Rose and Crown is a very old inn actually in the Cathedral Close. I found it odd, when I first visited England years ago, to find commercial establishments cheek-by-jowl with the ecclesiastical buildings, but it made sense when I realized that most of the old cathedrals, including Sherebury, were monastic foundations. When pilgrims came to visit the Cathedral they would probably stay in the guest rooms of the monastery itself, but if there was an overflow for a major feast, they had to go somewhere. It was convenient to have an inn virtually on the doorstep. It was convenient for Alan and me, too, so we often dropped in for a drink or a meal. The proprietors, Greta and Peter Endicott, had become dear friends, as had their daughter Inga, her husband Nigel Evans, and their two adorable children, Nigel Peter and Greta Jane. We'd been travelling so much of late that we hadn't seen the kids for a while. 'Tell me, Greta,' I asked when we were settled at a table, 'how are your grand-children doing?'

It was a good thing there were only a handful of customers, because Greta could go on about her darlings for quite a time. 'They're both splendid! Greta Jane is already reading, though she's only just finished the infants' school. She's turning into an artist, making fantastic little clay sculptures. And oh, Nigel Peter is the lead treble in his school choir, and is going to audition for the Cathedral choir this summer!'

Her face glowed. Greta, in her middle age or beyond, is truly the most beautiful grandmother I've ever known. Of German origin, she has fair skin and hair, and if the hair is touched with grey now, and her face shows laugh lines, it only highlights the beauty. And when she's happy, her smile seems to light up the room.

'Taking after their parents, then. You must be very proud of them.'

'Too proud. Peter says I'm terribly boring on the subject. And here I am nattering on while you're parched with thirst. What can I bring you to drink?'

As the room began to fill with diners and Greta went back to her duties at the front desk, we basked in the comfort of familiar surroundings, superb food (the Endicotts have a French chef) and friends. 'You know, Alan, I love all of England. Well, all of the UK, really. And I've so enjoyed our travels. But hackneyed as it may sound, there truly is no place like home.'

'Be it ever so humble,' he agreed, raising his glass of lovely old claret over his plate of Tournedos à la Bordelaise.

* * *

We walked home past the floodlit Cathedral, its protective presence seeming to hover over all of Sherebury, wrapping us in serenity. 'It's hard to believe anything terrible could happen here,' I said with a happy sigh.

Alan forbore to remind me of the many crimes he had dealt with in this city and county and even in this Cathedral, latterly with my help, but I could often read his mind, too. 'Oh, okay,' I responded to his silent comment, 'all's well for now, anyway. Thank you for not bursting my bubble.'

'And speaking of bubbles,' he said, opening our front door, 'you haven't forgotten, have you, that Lucy is arriving at the end of next week?'

'Oh, good grief, I had forgotten! And there's so much to do! The guest room hasn't been touched in weeks, and there's nothing in the fridge but leftovers, and—'

'Peace, woman. You know Ada Finch will do her usual painstaking job with the cleaning, and if you need help with the catering, Jane hasn't lost her touch with good plain British food. And if you truly believe you can't handle it, do you think the Endicotts would turn her away?'

'Yes, of course you're right. It's just that I don't even know the girl, and she might be the picky kind, or the sort that wants everything to be exactly like it was back home . . .' I ran down, quelled by Alan's smile and slowly shaking head. 'I'm dithering, aren't I? Amn't I?'

'However you phrase it, yes, you are. Sit down with a cat or two, and I'll make tea.'

He put more wood on the fire and stirred it up, while I reflected for the thousandth time on my great good fortune in husbands. Frank was a dear, and I'll always love him, and Alan is equally wonderful, but in different ways.

He's so very English, for one thing. Look at his impulse to make tea when I'm upset. Or ply me with food, or wine or bourbon, but always tea when push comes to shove. I'd never, in America, thought of tea as a cure-all, but I've come to accept the idea here, and even to admit it works. Maybe it isn't so much the tea as the loving care.

Then there's his chivalrous streak. He wants to protect me from the big, bad world. Which is sweet, but irritating at times.

I'm an independent-minded woman who likes to go her own way. We've argued this out over the years and compromised. I've agreed that I won't deliberately walk into danger and will always ask for his help when I need it. He's accepted my firm belief that I can look after myself, and has promised never to forbid any course of action he regards as risky.

And we usually stick to our promises.

Alan returned with the tea tray and a parade of animals. The cats were following in hopes of some milk, and Watson on the general principle that humans are often a source of food or amusement, and always of love. He's a big sloppy dog, mostly spaniel (according to Alan), and utterly devoted to both of us, but especially Alan.

'So have you worked out a plan of action, love?' said my spouse as he handed me a cup of tea and poured one for himself.

'Not really. I don't know what Lucy's schedule is, for one thing. Will she be occupied at the college – sorry, university – most of the time?'

'I don't know. The conference starts Monday morning and she's arriving at Gatwick very early on Saturday, so she'll get here around noon that day.'

'Are we to pick her up?' I said with some apprehension. I hate going anywhere near an airport, any airport.

'No, she's hiring a car. And before you start fussing about her getting lost, she told me she's relying on satnav, not her foggy memory of the area. And she'll have her mobile, and both of our numbers, and she assured me she is perfectly able to look after herself. Sound familiar?'

'Oh my, she has imbibed the American spirit, hasn't she? I begin to think we're going to get along just fine.' I looked at my cup of tea. 'Do you suppose a drop of brandy in this would lay me out, on top of all the alcohol I've already imbibed this evening?'

'Already in there, love. Drink it while it's still hot.'

'Weeping may spend the night, but joy comes in the morning,' says the Psalmist. A trifle optimistic, perhaps, but it's amazing how often it's true. Given a good night's sleep and a pleasant dawn, I'm almost always ready to be up and doing, with a heart for any fate.

Or if perhaps not quite that gung-ho, at least ready to take on the duties of the day.

The first of those, as soon as I'd downed a couple of cups of Alan's excellent coffee and some toast and marmalade, was to phone Ada Finch. Ada is our cleaning lady, or 'cleaner' in Britspeak. I met her quite literally over a body, and we've been friends ever since. Her son Bob, who has a bit of a drinking problem, is an excellent gardener when sober, and keeps my garden looking like an English dream. With their help I'm able to keep our four-hundred-year-old house looking the way it should.

It's not just a matter of appearance. Our house was built as a gatehouse when the monastery buildings were emptied by Henry VIII's Dissolution. He deeded the house to one of his friends for 'favours received'. It was then used as a home, with the Cathedral as a private chapel. As the years passed and politics changed, what was left of the monastery reverted to the Church of England, but the gatehouse remained a private residence and in due time was rented to my first husband when we decided to retire and move to England. Frank died before that could happen, but I kept the house and later Alan and I bought it.

We both love it, but upkeep is a constant chore, and as the house is a 'listed building' (something like a historic monument in America), the work must be done in accordance with various strict rules. Much as I'd love the convenience of modern double-glazed windows to replace the lovely diamond-paned ones that are so hard to keep clean, it can't be done, and we wouldn't really want to even if it were allowed. Both of us feel strongly that this house isn't exactly ours. It belongs to England; we're just temporary caretakers.

'Oh, hi, Ada. It's Dorothy. Are you at home or out on a job?'

'At 'ome restin' me pegs. Me rheumatics is flarin' up agin.'

'Oh, I'm sorry.' My heart sank. Without her help, I'd be hard put to get everything in order on time. 'Is Dr Wells able to help at all?'

An unmistakable snort came down the line. 'Doctors! Never

did set any store by them pills and such they give you. It's just this weather, but now spring's on its way, I'll be up an' about in no time. You'll be needin' me to 'elp get the 'ouse in order for that American girl oo's comin'.'

I wasn't even surprised that she knew about it. I learned long ago that the Sherebury grapevine was more efficient at gathering news than AP, Reuters, and Tass put together.

'It's a week tomorrow she's comin', right?' Ada continued. 'An' today's Friday. I'll send Bob to you tomorrow to get a start on them flahs, an I'll come in Monday mornin'.'

'But are you sure you'll feel up to it? I won't have you wearing yourself to a frazzle if—'

'An' since when can't I clean your 'ouse with one 'and tied behind me back? Frazzle, me eye!'

She wasn't really annoyed with me, and she knew I knew it. We both enjoyed this little game, along with the frequent cups of tea we drank together whenever she came over.

'Well, if you're sure, then I'll see you on Monday. And Bob tomorrow. That is . . . is he—?'

''E's been on the wagon fer a month now. I'll see 'e stays there till 'e finishes wiv your garding. Cheers, luv.'

Ada Finch, bless her, was one of those sturdy, determined women who have been the backbone of England since the beginning of time. Indomitable, opinionated, loyal, and strong as the English oak, she and her kind shore up the nation. I love her, and I would never, never want to get on her wrong side.

Another such was Jane Langland, my next-door neighbour. She has always reminded me of Winston Churchill, both in appearance and in her gruff speech. Her demeanour is, however, a pose hiding the kindest heart I know. She'll do anything for her friends and refuse to be thanked. As with Ada, though, anyone who offends her sense of justice will be given no quarter. She taught school for years in Sherebury, so there's almost no one who doesn't know and love her. And she's helped me out of I can't count how many scrapes.

I started to phone her, but looking out the window I saw she was just starting off for a walk with her bulldogs. They

all look exactly like her, and behave like her, too. Lots of bark
and no bite, but they intimidate my animals, so I make sure
my menagerie is inside when the dogs are out.

I ran out the back door. 'Jane, hold up! Can I come with
you?'

'Don't know. Can you?'

'Stop being pedantic. But "may I", if it makes you happier.'

'Either way.' She handed me some treats and a leash, fortunately of one of the smaller, less obstreperous beasts. 'Here.
Won't give you much trouble.'

'Is this Lola?'

A snort. 'Never did know much about dogs, did you? He's
Sam.'

'I just don't think it polite to examine their . . . er . . .'

Another snort. 'Doubt they'd mind. Heel, Rupert! Fool
dog.'

Sam turned to look at me, and I'd swear his expression was
a smug 'I'm being a good dog, I am!'. I grinned back and
slipped him a treat.

We walked along relatively peacefully, the dogs of course
sniffing every bush, fence post, and tree, and occasionally
getting their leashes tangled. Jane scolded and snorted, and
the dogs, knowing perfectly well that she adored them, took
little notice.

'They really are remarkably well-behaved, Jane. I don't
know how you do it.'

She ignored that, as she always ignores praise. 'Hear you're
having a visitor from America. One of Alan's relations?'

'Sort of. I'm not quite sure I have it straight, but it involves
an "honorary aunt". That was Helen, so of course Alan is an
honorary uncle. Or great-uncle. Or something.'

'Hmph. She want something?'

'That's just what we don't know. She's running a conference
at the university for a week, but that doesn't quite explain why
she's acting so effusive about seeing Alan. She scarcely knows
him after so many years away, and they were never all that
close.'

Jane waited. She knows me very well.

'Actually, I was hoping you might help me entertain her.'

He nodded. 'It may be nearly noon before we see her. So we've plenty of time.'

He reached for me, but I rolled away. 'None of that! I'm thoroughly awake now, thanks to you. And feeling wonderful, but I'm heading to the shower.'

His grumbling was good-natured.

I had planned a salad lunch, but the weather had turned chilly and the rain persisted. '"Oh, to be in England, now that April's there",' I sourly quoted Browning as I surveyed my resources for soup-making.

A tap at the back door, and Jane stepped into the kitchen. 'Thought you might like this. Beastly day.' In one hand she held a large bail-handled pot, in the other a carrier bag with something fragrant inside. She looked quite a lot like Paddington Bear, her yellow slicker dripping on the floor.

'Jane, you're soaked! Come in and have a cup of tea.'

'No. Muddy boots.' She set the pot on the nearest surface and handed me the carrier bag. 'Mulligatawny,' she said, pointing to the pot, and was out the door before I could even thank her.

The bag proved to contain a large, crisp-crusted cottage loaf, still warm. There was lunch, with no effort on my part. Truly, Jane is a saint.

Maybe it was Jane's kindness, or the lovely aromas of curry and fresh bread, or perhaps those 'possibilities', but I'd completely recovered from my heebie-jeebies by the time Lucy knocked on our door.

'Whew!' she said as she walked in the door. 'I know for sure I'm back in England! I can't imagine why I didn't bring an umbrella. And am I glad to be out of that car! I was too young when we left England to learn how to drive on the left, and all this' – she gestured to the grey, rainy world – 'sure didn't help the visibility any. But I managed, with only one or two dicey moments. And I'm sorry, I should have introduced myself before venting! I'm Lucy Bowman, and of course you're Dorothy Nes— I mean Martin!'

So this was Alan's quiet, sensible child! Well, the years do change people, especially the years from early adolescence to adulthood. Whatever she had been like then, now she was a lovely woman, tall and slender. Her black hair, streaming water, was in striking contrast to her Paul-Newman-blue eyes. But her most notable characteristic was her open, confident, yes 'bubbly' personality. I was won over immediately.

I laughed at her exuberance. 'My dear, I'm very happy to meet you. No, I won't give you a hug until you get out of that raincoat and dry off a bit.' Alan, helpful as always, was standing ready with a thick towel. 'And take those sopping shoes off. Maybe my slippers will fit you, or if not, a pair of socks. And what would you like to drink before lunch? I can offer almost anything from wine to bourbon to brandy, or tea or coffee if you'd prefer something hot.'

'Are tea and brandy mutually exclusive? Oh, I know I should be all polite and say anything would be great, but that's really no help, is it? And anyway, you're American, even if you sound like a Brit, and you don't seem like the kind to stand on ceremony.'

'Tea and brandy, it is, and it'll be ready as soon as you are. Upstairs with you now; Alan will show you your room.'

He and I exchanged a glance as they left the room. His eyebrows raised in question; I replied with a nod and smile. All was well.

I'm not sure Lucy stopped talking at all during lunch. She managed somehow, though, to ingest two large bowls of soup and about half the bread, slowing down only when I offered some cookies from my freezer.

'I couldn't eat another bite,' she said with a sigh. 'You're a terrific cook.'

'I cannot tell a lie. My next-door neighbour made everything. I don't do English cooking very well.'

'She's superb at American food, though,' Alan put in. 'We thought perhaps you'd like something you haven't been eating for the past several years.'

'I do miss English food sometimes, but I live near Chicago, you know, where you can get any kind of food, from any country in the world, so when I'm dying for some toad-in-the-hole or a Scotch egg, I can find it.'

'A little home food, eh?'

'Uncle Alan, to tell the truth, I don't know where home is anymore. When we first moved to America, I was so homesick for England I cried for weeks. But then things began to feel familiar, and the accent began to sound almost normal. And then my parents died and my world changed again. I didn't have a home then, not really. A student apartment isn't home, and I had no family. Then I got this great job, and I live in a nice place, but all by myself, except for a cat. I had to leave her with my boss and I miss her already.'

Alan's face took on a look of concern, but before he could speak, Lucy smiled.

'Oh, gosh, that sounds like a pity party, doesn't it? I didn't mean it that way, honestly. It's just the truth. I'm sort of a woman without a country. *But!*' She said it emphatically. 'That's about to change! I'm going to be an American for real one of these days. I've met this awesome guy, and he's asked me to marry him!'

I gave Alan a smug 'told you so' look, and said, 'How exciting! Tell us all about him! But don't start for a minute; I want to put the coffee on.' I had a feeling we were going to need it. Lucy was dying to sing the praises of her fiancé, and she'd probably keep going until jet lag caught up with her.

'Oh, I don't know where to start! His name is Iain, spelled with the second "i". Scotch, of course, only way back. And he's totally gorgeous. I'm dying to see him in a kilt sometime! Tall, tanned, blue eyes, great muscles – a maiden's dream! But that's not the best part. He's really, really smart, and – wait for it – he thinks it's great that I am, too! The first man I ever met, actually, who doesn't think women should be decorative and slightly stupid and submissive!'

I nodded in sympathy. 'Most of them were like that when I was young, too. I loved math when I was in high school, and I was good at it. I'd have loved to take more, trig and calculus and all that, but in those days girls weren't supposed to be good in any of the sciences, and I didn't have the courage to buck the rules. I've often wondered how rich I'd be if I'd gone into higher math and then computer science, which was just in its infancy back then. Though I loved teaching, and I've had a good life, and I'd probably never have met Frank if I'd taken the other path, so . . .' I shrugged.

'And just think of the horrid possibility that you might never have met *me!*' Alan did his best imitation of a chest-pounding gorilla.

'There's that,' I agreed. 'What a catastrophe! But I'm sorry, Lucy. I interrupted. What does this very, very smart young man do?'

'He's in fundraising, too, but for his own foundation. He's a very warm person, very compassionate, and he's worried for a long time about all the people who lost their jobs, their homes, everything they had, in the Covid pandemic. He isn't rich himself, but he knows a lot of people who are, and he got together with them and started the Foundation for Covid Philanthropy to help those poor people rebuild their lives.' She paused for breath. 'It's working, too. He's got scads of applications for the grants, and they've already given away thousands, mostly to families who lost a breadwinner to the pandemic.'

'His friends must be very wealthy, indeed,' commented Alan rather drily. 'And extremely generous.'

'Not all that wealthy. Not in the Bezos-Gates class. See, that's the beauty of it! Iain isn't just smart and nice, he's a financial wizard, too. He's been investing the donations in funds with good, solid returns, and it's those returns that build up the foundation and then go out to the applicants. And as soon as I get back home, I'm going to invest in the foundation myself. I'm certainly not rich, but I do have some savings, and it feels really good to know that Iain can make that grow into enough to actually help people!' Suddenly she yawned. 'Oh, sorry! I didn't mean to do that. But I guess it's been a long day. I can never sleep on planes.' She yawned again.

'Right,' I said, standing up. 'You need a nap. Not a long one, or you'll never get back on UK time. I'll let you sleep for two hours, and then we'll take a walk. If it's still raining, we'll sprint over to the Cathedral and walk there.' I gave her a hug and a pat. 'Scoot! I'll wake you at' – I looked at the kitchen clock – 'four on the dot. Sleep well.'

When she was out of earshot I looked at Alan. 'Am I wrong, or is there a distinct smell of rat? Maybe a Ponzi sort of rat?'

'I don't think you're wrong. But we both might be imagining things. I'm going to do a little investigating. Meanwhile, that nap sounds like a good idea for us, too.'

'Mm. I'd better set the alarm. The way I feel right now, I could sleep till midnight.'

'It's that sort of day. Let's enjoy a little leisure while we can.'

FOUR

I t was still rainy and cold and generally nasty when we woke up. But we all needed some exercise, so we bundled up in rain gear and splashed across the Cathedral Close. For once I didn't wear a hat. No point in letting the rain spoil it.

It was nearly time for Evensong, so there was a verger guarding the door, ready to turn away anyone who wanted just to tour the church, a no-no when a service is going on. In this weather there weren't very many tourists, and he knew us, so he just smiled at us and pointed the way to the choir, which of course we know very well. The poor man had to do something to feel useful.

The men-and-boys choir is one of the glories of almost any cathedral in the UK, but especially of ours. Our organist-choirmaster is a superb musician who manages to demand near-perfection without antagonizing the singers; a neat trick, particularly with the boys. They may look and sound like the angelic host, but no one who knows them would describe them thus. They range in age from seven to twelve or thirteen, when the voice breaks, and are all very bright, the better to think up new devilment.

They all also have perfect pitch, and the stars – the trebles – have that heart-breaking clarity of tone that sends me straight to cloud nine.

No matter that the presider was one of my least favourite canons, nor that there were very few people in attendance. The beautiful words and the beautiful music in the sublime setting were what I came for, and I was carried away as usual.

When it was all over and we had quietly left our pews, Alan let me come back to earth slowly, as he always did. He's a very understanding man who also finds the service moving. 'Right, then, love. Shall we walk around and show Lucy the best bits, or would you rather do that on a brighter day?'

'Oh, on a brighter day, please!' said Lucy. 'I remember some of my favourites, but I'd rather meet them again when I can really see them. If that's okay with you, Uncle Alan?'

Alan queried me with his eyebrows.

'I agree. I love this place when it's all dim and shadowy, but I admit it shows to better advantage with the sun coming through those glorious windows. Anyway I'm getting hungry. Lucy, would you rather have a real evening meal a bit later at the Rose and Crown, or a magnificent tea now at Alderney's?'

'Oh, tea, please! Then I'll know for sure I'm back in England! Do I remember some incredible toasted tea cakes?'

'You do. My absolutely favourite pastry. Onward!'

The tea rooms of England, once ubiquitous, have slowly vanished, victim to the increasingly frantic pace of modern life. Few people have time anymore to stop in mid-afternoon for a leisurely break of tea and pastries and chat. Still fewer view with favour the highly calorific pastries. In cathedral towns, though, the pace is slower. The residents tend to be older, and retired. Tourists flood the place in season, which these days lasts almost year-round. So, although lovely places like Alderney's fared badly during the pandemic shutdown, most of them survived and are now thriving, serving the clientele that missed them sorely when they were unavailable.

Even in the awful weather – perhaps *because* of the awful weather – a good number of people had made for the comfort of a good fire, good food, and steaming tea. Our favourite table was available, though, so we were soon settled with a lavish meal of sugar and fat and carbohydrates. 'Here's to indulgence!' I proclaimed, raising my teacup. The others, mouths already full, just nodded.

Alan waited until we had made substantial inroads on the toasted tea cakes and scones and tiny sandwiches and lemon tarts, and then smiled at Lucy and said, 'My dear, I was so interested in what you told us about Iain – what's his surname, by the way?'

'Campbell. Hard to get more Scotch than that, isn't it? But he was born in North Carolina. His parents were born there, too, but I guess his grandparents and on back were from farther north, in the mountains of Pennsylvania.'

'Appalachians, maybe?' I commented. 'There were a lot of Scottish settlers there in the eighteenth century.'

'I don't know if they go back that far,' said Lucy doubtfully. 'But a long way, anyway. His mom teaches at a university there, and his father works for the Biltmore Company. You know Biltmore?' she asked me.

'Heavens, yes! A stately home, Alan, much newer than any English ones, but certainly comparable. Built by the Vanderbilts – you've heard of them, surely.'

'Indeed. Fabulously wealthy family. Railways, wasn't it? And one of them married the Duke of Marlborough. She brought a lot of good healthy dollars into that somewhat impoverished family.'

I nodded. 'Oh, yes, I'd forgotten that. And yes, the fortune did begin with the railroads – ways – but then they branched out. Anyway, the house is amazing, and the gardens . . . well, I'll never forget them. What does his father do there, Lucy, do you know?'

'Fundraising.' She giggled. 'Like father, like son. See, even the Vanderbilt fortune isn't enough to keep Biltmore going. It's the largest house in America, and as Aunt Dorothy says – you don't mind if I call you "aunt", do you? I mean, you're Uncle Alan's wife . . .?'

'I don't mind at all, dear. Proceed.'

'Well, the house and the gardens are *huge*! So it takes hundreds of people to run the place, and even with something like a million tourists kicking in their entry fees every year, money simply *flies* out the door. And it all comes from the family fortune and private donations. No grants, no public money at all.'

'Admirable,' said Alan. 'The taxpayers have quite enough demands on their money. But you mentioned the Biltmore Company?'

'Well, see, there's a lot more to the estate than just the house and gardens. There are inns and hotels and a winery and I don't know what all, so the Biltmore Company is sort of the central authority that runs them all and hires the employees and all that. The point is, Biltmore is big business, and Mr Campbell is in charge of raising funds to keep it going.'

'And I suppose it's from his father that Iain learned his business expertise,' I said.

'That's where he got his start, and then he studied business and finance in college, and then got an MBA at Northwestern.'

'Master of Business Administration,' I translated for Alan. 'Northwestern University in Chicago. Highly respected school. Is that how you met him, Lucy? Some intermural business conference or something?'

'No, actually, it was pure chance. There was this Monet exhibition I wanted to see at the Art Institute, their own and a lot of borrowed ones from other museums. I *love* the Impressionists!'

'I believe the Art Institute of Chicago has one of the world's best collections of them,' Alan put in, giving me a smug grin as I was about to offer instruction to him – again. 'You know, love, I did visit America several times on police business, before I knew you. And I'm not entirely without cultural interests.'

Lucy giggled. Well, I suppose it was funny to her, two grey-haired dodderers trying to one-up each other. I quirked my eyebrows at her, and she continued. 'So I was standing there looking at the haystack paintings. There were three of them, just slightly different, and I stepped back a little to compare them better, and ran right into him! He was doing the same, stepping back from the garden painting behind me. So of course we apologized and all that, and then we both began to laugh so hard that the guard was giving us very unfriendly looks, so we left the gallery and Iain took me down to the basement café for a cup of coffee, only it turned out to be a glass of wine and then a sandwich and another glass of wine. We sat there for hours, until the museum was starting to close, and then we went out to find something to nosh on, but it was pouring! It had been coming down for quite a while, because there were huge puddles everywhere, and we didn't have umbrellas, so we just dashed across the street and up to the first place we came to, which was that Russian tea place – do you know it?'

I nodded; Alan shook his head.

'They've redecorated – it's really elegant. And they have really great Russian food. And vodka! And they were really crowded, because of the rain, so we sat at the bar and had some appetizers and vodka and talked some more, until the rain stopped and we walked down the Miracle Mile, just . . . dreaming.'

The end of the story was becoming apparent. 'And you ended up at his apartment,' I said, trying not to sound judgmental. She was a grown woman, for heaven's sake, and I wasn't her mother.

'No! That was the best thing of all! He was a perfect gentleman. He asked me for my address and phone number, so I gave him my card, and he put me in a cab, and gave the driver a bunch of money. And then he kissed me and sent me off home! Now what do you think of that!'

'I think he must be an extraordinary young man,' said Alan. 'And of course you saw more of him.'

'He called the next day and asked if I wanted to go to the Planetarium. I couldn't that day, I had to work, but we went the next weekend. And then to the zoo – both of them – and the symphony and the ballet – everything! We love all the same things, and we love being together! And then he gave me this!' She pulled up the silver chain around her neck and showed us the ring that had been hidden under her blouse.

It was stunningly familiar. I gasped. 'It's Diana's ring!'

Lucy laughed. 'Well, Kate's wearing that now, isn't she? But yes, this is a copy. Of course Diana died when I was just a baby, but I've always idolized her, and Iain says my eyes are just like hers, so he wanted to give me this to match them.'

It certainly did that. The sapphire was the same deep blue, and the surrounding diamonds looked like miniature stars, also very much like her eyes. 'But why aren't you wearing it on your hand?' I asked.

The stars dimmed. 'It's his parents. They don't want him to be engaged just yet.'

'But surely . . . how old is he?'

'Twenty-six. Just a year older than me.'

'And he's living on his own, and has a good job and big plans – so why on earth? Oh, I'm sorry, Lucy. It's none of my business. Forgive me.'

'No, it's a good question. I don't know why, myself. I've never met them, so it isn't a question of hate at first sight, or anything like that. But Iain says his father is adamant that we wait. It has something to do with business. I don't really understand it. But anyway, we *are* engaged, and we'll tell them when it seems like the right time. Of course he doesn't see a lot of them. Asheville's a long way from Chicago, and everyone's tied down to their jobs. Anyway, I'm going to wear it while I'm here. Nobody will notice, and it makes me feel good.'

'I hate to contradict a lady,' said Alan, who had been checking nearby tables to see if anyone was paying attention, 'but everyone will notice. You can't walk around flashing a thing like that, even without its associations, without attracting attention. I don't mean to seem mercenary, but is it insured?'

'Actually, no. That's another reason Iain doesn't want me to wear it openly. There are some neighbourhoods in Chicago . . .'

'And in England, too,' said Alan firmly. 'And then there's the question of customs. Did you declare it when you came in?'

'Oh, dear! No. It never occurred to me. I just walked through the "nothing to declare" lane, and nobody paid any attention to me.'

'That could pose a problem when you leave the country.

You see, you didn't officially bring it in to the UK. Smuggling valuable goods is frowned upon, you know.'

'But – but I didn't smuggle anything! You believe me, don't you?'

'Of course I do, but it was an unwise thing to do, child. And it's still more unwise to wear it on your finger, with no insurance.'

'I can see that, now. But I do want to wear it, and I won't have time to do anything about a valuation and insurance. Tomorrow's Sunday, and I'm due at the university first thing Monday morning. I guess I'll just have to hide it again. Drat!'

'My dear, will you allow me to look into the matter? I would be happy to take the ring for a valuation and then see about insuring it. A short-term policy shouldn't be terribly expensive.'

She hesitated. 'I hate to give it up, even for a little while – but that's just silly. It's what it stands for that's important. And you're right. It's foolish to risk theft. I'll wear it to church tomorrow – hidden! – and then hand it over. You will take great care of it, won't you?'

'You may be sure of that,' Alan promised her. 'Now would you like a little supper, or would you rather go back home and watch television? If there's anything worth watching.'

'To tell the truth, I'd rather just go to bed. That nap didn't make much of a dent in the sleep deprivation. And I guess we'll need to get up sort of early?'

'No later than seven, if you want to go to the early service. If you'd rather wait a bit, Matins is at ten, followed by the sung Eucharist.'

'I'll probably wake up early. Still on Chicago time. But I do want to go to Matins. That taste of an English church choir this evening just whetted my appetite for more!'

After we'd got her settled, Alan and I went back downstairs for a nightcap. He poured us both a small bourbon and sat down with me in front of the fire, for the weather was still most un-springlike, even though May was just over a week away.

'You're up to something,' I said quietly.

'Why would you think that?' He tried to sound innocent, but we've been married too long for him to get by with much.

'You know perfectly well that the customs people wouldn't raise a fuss over a ring she brought into the country in perfect innocence. She'd have no trouble at all proving it was hers.'

'Probably. On the other hand, it's quite true that a little bauble like that is a positive invitation to a thief. It should be insured.'

'But that's not the only reason you want to get your hands on it.'

His face looked exactly like Emmy's when she's been raiding the pantry. 'You do have a suspicious mind, my dear.'

'Usually justified.'

His only reply was a smile.

FIVE

Sunday proceeded in its usual peaceful order. We're so used to the church bells almost overhead that we hardly hear them anymore, but I'd forgotten to warn Lucy. At any rate, when Alan and I got downstairs we found a note on the breakfast table. 'Bells woke me. What a great way to start a day! I went to early service; be back soon. Coffee pot's ready to turn on.'

'Iain's a lucky man,' I commented, starting the coffee.

Alan said, 'Toast or cereal?'

We never have much of a breakfast on Sunday, knowing we'll have a big noon meal. Lucy came in as we were munching our toast. 'That was awesome,' she said with a happy sigh. 'I'm glad I waited to see the Cathedral in daylight. I'd truly forgotten how the light comes in through the stained glass and puddles on the floor in rainbows. Can I make myself some toast? I'm starving.'

'Of course you are,' said Alan, starting to get up. 'You need a proper breakfast. You must have been up for hours.'

She waved him back to his seat. 'No, toast and coffee will be fine. There isn't time for eggs and all that. Yeah, I was awake even before the bells started, but they got me out of bed, for sure! How do you live with all that racket?'

'"The one loud noise made to the glory of God",' I quoted Dorothy Sayers. 'We're so used to them that we seldom hear them anymore, unless they're ringing a peal, or practising for one. Now you're sure you want to come to Matins with us? It makes a bit of a rush on Sunday morning, and you're quite free to do as you please.'

'And what I please, Aunt Dorothy, is to go to church with you.'

'Don't fuss, love,' said Alan. 'The girl knows her own mind. Just finish your coffee, both of you, and see to your lipstick, or whatever touching up is needed. The five-minute bell is just about to begin its pious summons.'

After the service we had a cup of stewed tea in the parish house, which had once been the scriptorium when the Cathedral was an abbey, in the fifteenth century. Somehow the despoilers over the years hadn't damaged it structurally, and with additions of such anachronisms as electricity and rudimentary plumbing and slightly more comfortable furniture, it served reasonably well for parish meetings and so on. On Sunday mornings the congregation gathered there for tea or coffee (neither really drinkable) and pastries rather past their prime. The real menu, of course, was gossip. Cathedral towns batten on gossip, most of it harmless. The Cathedral coffee hour was the nerve centre of the Sherebury grapevine (to mix metaphors).

Alan and I often skipped it, but this morning I wanted to introduce Lucy to my friends. Jane, of course, sized her up with one penetrating glance and nodded. 'Glad to meet you. Knew your grandmother. Good woman. You're like her.'

And that, for Jane, was an A-plus approval rating.

Lucy gaped as Jane turned away. 'My mom used to say I was like Grandma, but how on earth could Miss Langland tell? I don't look like her.'

'Jane Langland taught school for even more years than I

did. One learns a lot about people that way. I could identify an eleven-year-old darling, or a big-time troublemaker, the first time they entered my classroom. If she says you pass muster, you can consider yourself highly praised.'

'Hmm. It's kind of scary to be that transparent.'

'You wouldn't be to everybody,' I assured her. 'But never try to keep a secret from Jane.'

The dean and his wife were cordially welcoming, as were Nigel Evans and his family. The Endicotts weren't there, as Sunday lunch was imminent at the Rose and Crown, and they were busy with preparations, but any number of other people came to greet us. Sherebury is a small town, almost a village, though the august presence of the Cathedral affords it the superior designation of 'city'. But in all essentials, it's a village. Almost everyone knows almost everyone else, which can have its disadvantages if one is a private sort of person, but Alan and I are not, and we welcome the easy friendliness. It took me a while to be accepted at first, but now most of our neighbours have apparently forgotten that I'm an 'incomer', and treat me as one of their own. Of course marriage to Alan didn't hurt.

At any rate, by the time we strolled over to the inn for our meal, Lucy had met most of our friends and was, I hoped, feeling truly welcome.

Sunday afternoon proceeded as Sunday afternoons do. Sated with traditional Sunday lunch (including trifle), we walked home and took naps, even Lucy, who is young but was still catching up on her sleep. When we woke, the weather having reverted to proper spring, serene and smiling, we took a stroll through Sherebury, almost as far as the university.

'Where are your lectures being held?' Alan asked. 'Which building, I mean?'

'The Berwick Building. I think it's where the business school hangs out, but I don't know exactly where it is. They sent me a map, but I'm not too great at reading maps.'

'I know it,' said Alan. 'It's just on the edge of campus. One of the newer buildings. In fact' – he looked up, squinted, and pointed – 'that's it, there. The one that's nearly all glass.'

'Gosh! Looks more like an American hotel. Okay, I won't have trouble finding it tomorrow. What about parking?'

'Iffy,' I said with a grin. 'Like most places here. The English didn't plan their cities and universities in obeisance to the internal combustion engine.'

'Then I'll walk, if it doesn't rain. No, I can see you're about to offer me a ride, but I promised myself I wouldn't be a nuisance. If it's too wet to walk, I'll just call someone at the university and make them pick me up. I'm the honoured guest, after all!'

The moment Lucy was out of sight the next morning (having decided to walk, since the fair weather continued), Alan made a couple of phone calls and then picked up his hat. 'I'm off to London, love. Not sure when I'll be back, but not for lunch. I'll call.'

'You're going to London without me?' I was astonished. We do almost everything together, and Alan knows how much I love London.

'Sorry, but this isn't a pleasure trip. Anyway, you need to be here when Lucy returns. I'll tell you all about it when I get back.' He kissed me and headed out the door, leaving me staring after him. This must, I thought, have been what life was like for Helen, when Alan was a working policeman and often had to leave for parts unknown at no notice.

Well, but he wasn't a working policeman anymore. So why . . .?

It was futile to speculate with no data. And I needed to figure out what I was going to feed Lucy for lunch – if she was going to be here for lunch – and all of us for dinner.

She called to say she'd be back in the late afternoon. Apparently she was being taken out to lunch and later for tea. 'It's such fun!' she enthused over the phone. 'They're treating me like royalty.'

'Fundraising is important,' I pointed out. 'And you're good at it.'

'And I'm teaching them to be good at it, too. Oops, sorry Aunt Dorothy, gotta go.'

So everybody was off having a wonderful time. Great. I

was just about to work myself into a real snit when Watson made a fuss at the back door. When I opened it, he bounded in, greatly pleased with himself. He'd brought me a wonderful toy. Gently he put it down on the floor, licked it all over, and looked up at me for praise.

It was a very small, very bedraggled kitten, wet from Watson's well-meant attentions, and mewing unhappily.

I closed the kitchen door hastily. I wasn't sure where Sam and Emmy were, but the mews would bring them in a trice, and they wouldn't be pleased.

I got a towel, picked up the little mite, and said, 'Now what am I going to do with you? Do you belong to someone?'

Watson looked at me anxiously.

'Yes, you're a good boy,' I assured him, and gave him a loving pat. 'It's a fine kitty, but I hope you didn't steal him from a neighbour.'

Once the poor little thing was more or less dry, I got out some canned cat food, diluted it with a little warm water, and put it on the floor. I wasn't sure the kitten was old enough to eat solid food, but it settled right down and lapped happily. I found my phone, sat down and called Jane, and explained my dilemma. 'It's a pretty little thing, sort of a tortoiseshell, and I think it might be long-haired, though it's hard to tell – still sort of damp. Do you know where it belongs?'

'Dumped,' she said, a world of contempt in her voice. 'Saw the car, but couldn't catch the cat. Glad Watson did. A good dog.'

'Honestly, people who would do a thing like that . . . there are no words.'

'Like to dump *them* out of a car. In the rain. Or snow. It's a female, of course.'

'You know I'm no good at telling, especially when they're so young. But torties always are, aren't they?'

'Nearly.'

There was a pause. 'Jane, you know I can't keep her. Sam and Emmy would have a fit. They'd probably kill her, poor little thing.'

Another pause.

'Well, of course I won't turn her away until I've had her checked out. But then I'll have to find her a good home. Maybe Nigel and Inga.'

'Two dogs.'

'Oh, I forgot. Well, if you hear of someone who wants a lovely little kitten, let me know.'

'Mmm.'

I gave up and clicked off the phone. Plainly Jane wasn't going to be of any help. I looked down. Watson was sprawled at my feet, the kitten nestled between his paws. Both were sound asleep.

Oh, dear.

I made myself a hasty lunch of leftovers and then called my vet, a crusty Scotsman who was brusque with people and gently sweet with animals. Yes, he could see the kitten this afternoon, said his secretary, who was also brusque with people. She'd been suspicious of me ever since I brought Emmy in after seeing her lap up some antifreeze, years ago. Nothing could convince the secretary that my negligence hadn't been responsible for my cat's brush with death, though the vet had accepted that it was a case of deliberate poisoning.

The kitten was so small I didn't think I needed to put her in a carrier, so I took her away from Watson (with protests from both parties), tucked her under my arm, and made for the vet's office.

Where I met with a surprise. After he'd given the kitten a thorough exam and administered the necessary shots, I had a question for Mr Douglas. 'I suppose she's too young to be spayed yet, but how soon do you think—' I stopped. He was fixing me with a strange look.

'I'd say, never. Did ye not know the wee moggie's a male?'

'But . . . is it not a tortoiseshell, then?'

'Aye, he is. And unless he's sterile, as often happens, he's worth a good wee sum.'

I sat down. 'And someone dumped him. Just threw him out of a car. A beautiful, valuable cat.'

'Ye've got a treasure there, I hope ye know. Healthy, strong, sweet-tempered. I'll not be needin' to see much o' him, once he has all his jabs. Look after him well, mind.'

Oh, dear.

I did hope Alan would get home soon. I needed help in coping with this unexpected situation. It wasn't made any easier when the kitten settled down in the car and purred herself – himself – to sleep. This was an animal plainly well satisfied with the current state of affairs. And, to be honest, I had already fallen under his spell. Beautiful, soft, well-behaved – so far – I'd be happy to keep him. But how could I?

Watson was pacing unhappily when I got home, looking for his new friend. With the other cats nowhere to be seen, I put the kitten on the floor. He walked over to the dog (at least thirty times his size) and touched noses, purring. Watson licked him, overjoyed to see him again, and then they started to play, the cat batting at Watson's ears, Watson catching the kitten's tail and trying to hold it down. I was just wishing I knew how to make movies on my phone when trouble walked in, in the form of a very angry Esmeralda.

She stopped just inside the kitchen door. Every single grey hair was standing on end. Her back was arched, her tail bushed. In case somebody didn't get the point, she was hissing loudly, with an occasional growl.

The kitten, wide-eyed, scurried between Watson's paws. Watson, who usually took care not to annoy the cats, raised his head, looked Emmy in the eye, and barked. Once. Loudly. Then he nudged the kitten into a corner, stood up, and slowly advanced toward Emmy, growling low in his throat.

Now I know that it's folly to attribute human emotions and reactions to animals. But I'm prepared to swear that Emmy was quite simply astonished. When she and Watson had first met, she had established her pre-eminence with one swift scratch on the nose, and that was the end of it. She was the boss. Period. They became good friends, but Watson was always careful to observe the hierarchy.

Now here was this large friend acting like a dog! And a menacing dog at that. Some recalculation was required. Emmy didn't back down. Cats don't back down. She simply turned away, retired to the parlour, and began a thorough wash.

Meanwhile Sam had been watching the whole thing from

a safe distance. Her inscrutable Siamese face gave no hint of what she was thinking.

And the kitten? He yawned, showing very white teeth and a very red tongue, and went to sleep again, on Watson's back.

I shook my head and went back to thinking about the evening meal. I'd got as far as some smoked salmon to start, when Alan came home.

Before I could get a word in, Watson proudly dislodged the kitten, picked him up off the floor, and dropped him at Alan's feet. So I began to explain the whole sequence. 'And Watson's decided he's the baby's godfather, or nanny, or something. I'm hoping it will all work out, but—'

'Darling, I do want to hear the whole story, but it'll have to wait. I must talk to you before Lucy gets back.'

He sounded so upset that I shut up in mid-sentence. 'What's wrong?'

He dropped wearily into a chair. 'Lucy's ring is a fake.'

SIX

I just stared at him, mouth agape.

'That's what I've been doing, having it valued. I was pretty sure, having dealt with cases of insurance fraud. I'm no expert, of course, but I've seen enough paste to make a reasonable guess. The jeweller they consult at Scotland Yard says it's very good paste, very expensive. If the ring had been made in England, he says he could put a name to the maker. Apparently there are only a handful who can do such professional work. As it's from the States, he'd have to do a little research.'

'And it's worth . . .?'

'Probably five hundred pounds.'

'And if it were real?'

Alan shrugged. 'Diana's ring – Kate's, I should say – was recently valued at around three hundred thousand.'

'Pounds?'

Alan just nodded.

'Oh, poor Lucy! Not just the value. Not even mostly the value.'

'No. The fact that her fiancé deceived her. Of course, it makes one wonder what other deceptions he might have practised.'

The front door opened. 'Yoo-hoo! Anybody home?'

'Don't tell her,' I mouthed, just in time.

Watson did his act again: picked up the kitten, who by now was becoming used to it, and showed him proudly to Lucy as she came into the parlour. 'Well! Who's this sweet baby?'

So then I had to explain the whole thing again, including the parts I hadn't had time to tell Alan. Meanwhile Alan poured us all a drink and we sat watching the animals.

'So what's his name?' she asked.

Alan and I looked at each other. 'We haven't decided we can keep him,' I finally admitted. 'The other cats—'

'Oh, don't worry about them. They'll adjust. I've known lots of cats. They're the ultimate realists. Watson dealt with Emmy, you tell me, and Sam is too smart to rock the boat. The little guy's here to stay, but you can't keep calling him "the kitten". I think he should be Leonardo. Or maybe Michelangelo.'

'Why on earth?' I asked.

'He's a tortoiseshell. A tortoise is a turtle, more or less.'

We still looked blank.

'Oh, I forgot. You're the wrong generation. The Teenage Mutant Ninja Turtles are named after famous artists, I can't remember why. Raphael, Donatello, and the other two. I like Michelangelo, myself. You could call him Mikey. Or Mike. And it fits. Mike is the mischievous one of the group. The most kitten-like.'

'Mike.' I tried it out. 'Mike.'

And the kitten wriggled out from between Watson's protective paws, came over, climbed my slacks, and lay purring in my lap. That seemed to settle it.

I gave in with a sigh. 'The others aren't going to like it. They're used to having their humans all to themselves.'

'They accepted Watson,' Lucy pointed out.

'That's different from another cat.'

'It'll work out. Anyway, you're hooked, aren't you?'

I looked at the soft, warm little darling in my lap. 'I'm hooked.'

At our evening meal (my wonderful husband had brought home some sausages, so we had an easy bangers and mash supper), we listened to Lucy regale us with her day at the university.

'There's such a lot they need to know,' she said, 'and they're so eager to learn. You'd think it would be obvious to anyone that the tactics used to sell cars or cat food could, with modification, be used to sell a college to potential donors. But no. On this side of the pond it all has to be done discreetly, diplomatically, with no suggestion of any dog-and-pony shows. That's fine if you're Oxford or Cambridge, with benefactors lining up at the doors to give you money and gain recognition, but it isn't going to work at a small place like Sherebury.'

'Are you saying that the English are hidebound?' said Alan in mock resentment.

'I guess I am, because honestly, in some ways they are. And no, I haven't forgotten that I'm English, born right here in Sherebury, but by now I'm mostly American. I love the old, quaint stuff, don't get me wrong, but sometimes it drives me crazy!'

'That's because you're young,' I said pontifically. 'The young are always impatient. It's us old fogies who revel in "the way we've always done it".'

'You be careful who you're calling names, woman! I refuse to surrender to the accusation. It is not fogeyism to believe that things were often done better in the days of yore.' Alan attacked his sausage with vigour, propelling a jet of fat halfway across the table. Lucy and I giggled, and so, after a moment, did Alan.

'Truce,' I proclaimed, wielding my fork as a gavel. 'Now, what would you like for dessert? I can offer only store-bought biscuits – cookies, Lucy, in case you've forgotten – and or home-canned blackberries, courtesy of Jane. I was too busy to pick blackberries last fall, and they're not ripe yet this year, but I'm going to try to make a couple of cobblers this fall.'

And the conversation turned to the delights of seasonal fruits and vegetables, and then a fracas developed between the animals in the parlour, and we had to go and sort that out. Emmy, typically, declared herself the winner and stalked away, leaving little Mike unscathed and, so far as I could tell, unalarmed. Watson, of course, resumed his role of protector and nudged Mike off to a corner for thorough inspection and licking. The kitten tolerated the attention remarkably well and then proceeded to lick himself clean of the doggy smell.

'You do worry about so many things that never happen,' commented Alan. 'They're all going to get on together.'

'You're right. And I'll keep on worrying. It's in my DNA.'

'Speaking of worrying,' said Lucy, 'have you had time to get my ring valued and insured?'

I was afraid to look at my husband, but he was ready for the question. 'I did, and it's insured for its full value, but only for the next month. When you get home you'll have to do the whole thing all over again, I'm afraid. Meanwhile I'm happy to return it to you, but I still suggest you wear it on the chain, concealed. Insurance won't do you much good if some thief spots it when you're alone and decides it's worth injuring you, or worse.'

She sighed as he pulled it out of his pocket and handed it over. 'I suppose you're right. I guess it is a sort of liability. I'd never thought of that.' She slipped the chain over her head and tucked it under her shirt. 'How much did you have to pay for the insurance? I'll write you a cheque.' She reached for her purse and then hesitated. 'Oh, I forgot. A cheque in dollars won't do you any good, will it? Tomorrow I'll go to an ATM and get some pounds for you.'

'Don't worry about it, child. It cost very little for such a short time. You can buy us a splendid bottle of wine instead.'

She laughed. 'Mom said you always were an old smoothie. And I was going to give you some wine anyway, so there.'

'What's on your calendar for tomorrow?' I asked brightly, eager to keep her from returning to the subject of the ring.

'Same-old, same-old. Two lecture sessions in the morning, lunch with some bigwigs, discussion groups in the afternoon. I think I'll be done by teatime, though, and unless someone invites me to tea, I'd like to take you both to Alderney's.'

'We're all going to have to go on diets if we keep this up. Their teas, as you know, are not exactly "lite".' I made air quotes with my fingers. Emmy, who was sitting nearby studiously ignoring me, interpreted the gesture as an invitation and jumped heavily into my lap, securing her balance by firmly attaching her claws. She knows quite well that claws are not to be used on humans. She also knows that I would accept almost any token of reconciliation. I held up both hands in surrender. 'You,' I told her lovingly, 'are the most impossible beast I know.' I scratched her behind her ears, and she purred.

Peace reigned. We watched a little boring television, had a small nightcap each, and took ourselves off to bed.

Lucy was gone by the time Alan and I got out of bed in the morning. She had insisted that she didn't need to be pampered and was perfectly able to fix her own breakfast, and we took her at her word. We'd given her a key, so she could come back whenever she wanted.

After we'd had enough coffee to be more or less coherent, I brought up the ring. 'What are we going to do about it, Alan? Tell her and break her heart? Or let her find out when she gets home and has to confront him?'

'I'm less worried about the ring itself than what it implies. As I started to say yesterday, I'm wondering what else he's said or done that isn't true.'

'The smell of rat is getting stronger, isn't it? Is there more coffee?'

He got up and poured us both another cup. 'I'm troubled enough that I'd like to find out a great deal more about this young man. If he were English, it would be simple enough. But he isn't, and I can no longer ask Scotland Yard to look into the background of a foreigner against whom there is nothing but a vague feeling that something's not right.'

'And the ring.'

'And the ring. For which there might be a hundred innocent explanations.'

'Name one. I can't think of any.'

He grinned. 'That's because you don't have the criminal mind, my dear, as I've often said. But we're talking innocence here. He might be temporarily short of money, and bought this as a place-marker until some investment turns up trumps. He might have ordered a really lovely ring, the real McCoy, and it didn't come in time.'

'That's two, not a hundred, and I don't buy either of them. He's an investment banker, or something of the sort. He has access to lots of money, and could borrow against a forth-coming windfall. Besides, what was the hurry? He was under no pressure to pop the question at any particular time.'

Alan raised his eyebrows. 'Are you sure of that?'

'My dear man, I may never have been pregnant, but I have lots of nieces. I do know the signs. I'm quite sure. There is no question of a shotgun wedding. Trust me. So unless you can come up with another ninety-eight innocent explanations, at least one of which holds water, I'm sticking by my own interpretation. Which is that all is not as it should be. There's a rat i' the arras. I smell fish. Something wicked this way comes. Whatever metaphor you want. And what are we going to do about it?'

'What we're *not* going to do is launch an official investi-gation with all the bells and whistles. We can't, either of us. I no longer have the authority, and you never did.' He held up a hand as I started to protest. 'What we can do is use our contacts. I spent a fair amount of time in the States when I was chief constable here, and I've kept in touch with a number of the police officers I met over the years. They've almost all retired by now, of course, but they still have connections – as I do here. And you, of course, know any number of people, who know people, and so on. I propose that we start asking questions of anyone we can think of who might be able to tell us about one Iain Campbell.'

'You, my dear, are a genius! Of course I know people! Lots of Randolph University people, who can trace the academic end. And I have a dear friend in North Carolina who can get in touch with Biltmore. And—'

'I don't need the whole list, love. You have emails and phone numbers for these people, I hope? I think there may be some urgency about the matter.'

'Me, too.' I sobered rapidly. 'Yes, whatever's going on, it isn't pretty.' I glanced at the clock on the mantel. 'It's too early to call anyone over there, but I can send a couple of emails to people who always reply right away. That'll get the ball rolling.' I hesitated. 'And we're not going to talk to Lucy about any of this, right?'

'Not yet. I'll get on the phone as soon as it's a reasonable time in the States. We may be chasing a wild goose, to add to our metaphorical zoo, and there's no reason to alarm her until we're sure of our facts.'

Which just goes to show how wrong a couple of intelligent, well-meaning people can be.

SEVEN

Lucy didn't make it home for tea, but plodded through the door at about six and dropped, with a loud sigh, into the first chair that was handy.

Alan poured her a drink and waited until she'd downed a healthy swig before asking, 'Tough day?'

She nearly choked on her bourbon. 'You might say that,' she said when she had recovered. 'I don't know if I can survive much more English enthusiasm. You're all supposed to be laid-back and serene, but this crowd! I felt like a rock star being mobbed by fans. Oh, they were polite about it, of course. But they wouldn't let me leave. I had to plead an urgent appointment before I could get out the door.'

We must both have looked sceptical, because she took another gulp of her drink and said, 'You don't believe me. I wouldn't have believed it, either. I think they think I'm some kind of celebrity or something. I keep getting emails from people they think are important, so they – the conference attendees, I mean – have gotten it into their heads that I must be the world's authority on fundraising, and they seem to think if they stick to me like burrs something will rub off.' She finished the bourbon and set down her glass. 'I'd really like another, but maybe I'd better have something to nibble? I never did get any tea. Are there any crackers – biscuits, I mean?'

I scurried to the kitchen and brought back a box of assorted 'Drinks Biscuits' and a bowl. 'They're in various flavours, cheeses and herbs, and we think them quite tasty with bourbon or scotch or almost anything. Help yourself.' I dumped them into the bowl and set it near Lucy.

Alan had meanwhile refilled her glass with a rather paler mixture this time. She took a few biscuits from the bowl and sat back with a contented sigh. 'Now this aspect of Olde England I could get used to.'

'But you must tell us, Lucy, who these important people are who keep sending you messages.' Alan sounded really interested, for reasons which escaped me at the time.

'Oh, they're nothing to do with me, really. I mean I don't actually know any of them. They're just donors, and anyway it's their secretaries or lawyers or whatever who deal with me.' She ate a cracker or two, sipped her drink, and reeled off a list of names.

This time I was the one who choked. The combined net worth of the people whose names she was tossing around would have bought most of London, with enough left over for a village or three.

'I can see why your conference people are impressed,' said Alan moderately. 'How did they come to know about these messages?'

'That was me. Stupid, I guess, but I never thought anyone would be interested. The conference office printed them out for me, and I answered them as soon as I saw them. These people don't like to be kept waiting, you know, and they'd already waited a couple of hours.'

'You answered them how?' asked Alan, not quite so casually.

'On my phone, of course. Oh, you mean, did I type them

'Oh. Well, that isn't very helpful, is it?'

'Not very, no. Go to bed. We're both too tired to think properly. Morning will be better.'

Morning was awful. In the first place, the weather had reverted to nastiness. The rain wasn't cold, just relentless. The sky was that uniform grey that tells you the sun has no intention of ever shining again. There was just enough wind that, no matter how you held your umbrella, you got wet. The rain earlier in the week had saturated the ground, so there were puddles everywhere. The only saving grace was that the weather served as a good excuse for my unhappy mood.

I'm not sure Lucy even noticed, though. She was dancing on air and talking a blue streak about Iain's visit. There was little room for comment from Alan or me. She ate her usual modest breakfast and took off in her car, optimistic about finding a parking place. No walking today.

Jane and Dean Allenby were first on my agenda for the day, but the stars were aligned against me. Jane didn't answer her door (though a loud volley of barking did), and I remembered that she'd said she had a date in London to visit an old pupil's matinee performance in a new play. She probably wouldn't be home before Lucy. And the dean, his secretary told me, was in conference with some diocesan officials all morning. She was so sorry; she'd have him call me as soon as he was available. Meanwhile, could one of the canons be of service?

Well, no. I knew all the canons, of course, and liked most of them, but this matter required a friend. Required Jane or the dean, in short.

In the afternoon, reports began to come in from my American sources. My friend in Asheville said that the Biltmore Company hired out its fundraising operation. My friends in Frank's university in southern Indiana had not been able to find an Iain Campbell in the student records of any major institution of higher learning, and were now branching out to the smaller ones, but even if they limited the search to the Midwest, it might take some time. A genealogist friend simply sighed when I suggested searching for Campbells. 'Why not try John

Smith, while you're asking?' No, I didn't know where in Scotland the family might have originated. No, I didn't know if they had ever been involved in the manufacture of soup.

In short, I had nothing to add to Alan's dossier. The fact that we couldn't find traces of the young man, or his family, didn't prove anything, of course, even if it was suggestive. I was beginning to look forward to meeting this person so I could draw some conclusions for myself.

When Lucy came home, well before teatime, she was as excited as a six-year-old before her birthday party. She hadn't yet heard from Iain. 'They let me off my afternoon schedule to greet him. He should call soon,' she said. 'His taxi is probably tied up in London traffic.'

Alan looked at the clock and raised an eyebrow, but said nothing.

Lucy and I went out to the kitchen to prepare some titbits to go along with a welcoming drink. We fussed over them a bit, wanting them to be rather special. By the time they were ready and stored in the fridge, another hour had elapsed. No phone call.

Lucy was beginning to get edgy. 'I'd better call him. He might have lost your phone number.'

But he wouldn't have lost yours, I thought. It would surely be programmed into his phone.

She clicked off. 'I'm getting "out of service". He probably forgot to charge it, silly man. He'll show up soon, all apologies.'

But he didn't. When four o'clock rolled around we decided we might as well attack those nibbles ourselves, along with a glass of wine to settle our nerves. We had run out of excuses for Iain and couldn't seem to find anything else to talk about, so Alan switched on the news. Nothing there to ease our minds, of course. The usual natural disasters, riots in various parts of the world, Parliament fighting it out over old, stale issues.

'And this just in. A hit-and-run accident has left one man dead in London. According to witnesses, he was crossing Buckingham Palace Road near Victoria Station when a car, travelling at high speed, struck him with such force that he was thrown to the steps leading to the Grosvenor Hotel. The car did not stop, and no one noted the licence number. The victim, who was carrying an American passport, was pronounced dead at the scene. Further details will be released as available. Police are investigating.'

EIGHT

Lucy was pale and trembling. I poured a small tot of brandy and handed it to her. 'Get that down and try not to think the worst. How many thousand Americans do you suppose there are in London right now?'

She drank, silently, and some colour came back to her face, but she couldn't seem to stop shaking. I sat down on the arm of her chair and put my arm around her.

Alan had gone straight to his office and closed the door. I was sure he was checking for those 'details to be released later'.

He came back looking sombre. 'Description: six feet two inches; Caucasian, but very tanned skin; blue eyes, black hair; excellent physical condition. Recently arrived Heathrow from Chicago.'

He paused. Tears were streaming down Lucy's face.

'The name on the passport and on his ticket stub is William Gray.'

'But – but then it *isn't* Iain.' Lucy's voice was choked with tears. 'The description sounds like him, but . . .'

'Lucy,' said Alan, sounding very tired, 'if you'll come look at my computer for a moment . . .'

She rose unsteadily and went with him. I followed.

There on the screen was a passport, with a photo. Lucy took one look at it, gasped, and fell against Alan's arm.

We put her to bed. I wanted to call our doctor, but she refused so adamantly that I thought it best not to insist. I did call Jane, who came and talked soothing nonsense until Lucy cried herself to sleep. Kenneth Allenby came, murmured a prayer, and joined us all in the parlour.

'This might be a blessing,' I said with a sigh. 'Alan, you tell them while I make tea.'

Good grief, I thought, I'm converting to Alan's English mindset, turning in a true crisis to tea as the panacea. I returned with a tray in time to hear Alan say, 'And I suppose now I understand why we could find no trace of him anywhere he said he had been. He was operating under a false name. That is, I'm assuming the passport is genuine. It's not at all easy to get a passport under an assumed name.'

'It's easier in America, I think, or at least it used to be. They may be more careful now. But in any case, if you were a con artist and had to choose between your drab real name, William Gray, and a flashy name like Iain Campbell, which would you choose?' I set the tray down and poured out for everyone, helping myself to several biscuits from the box. 'Sorry, but we missed our tea.'

'And your theory about this young man is?' asked the dean.

I nodded to Alan.

'We think he was operating a fraudulent scheme under the guise of a charity. I can't provide any details. We will have to get those from the States and, I fear, from poor Lucy.'

'Means you'll have to tell her,' said Jane gruffly.

I had just realized that. 'Yes, I'd hoped that we could just sympathize and all, but she'll have to know. If for no other reason . . .' I looked at Alan.

'Yes. The hit-and-run will have to be thoroughly investigated. Given his probably criminal pursuits, there's at least some possibility that it was no accident. I called the Yard while you were ministering to Lucy,' he added, 'and told them most of what I know, including his alias. They'll be working with the Chicago police, of course. I have the hideous feeling that this could blow up to be something very nasty, indeed.'

'Meanwhile,' I added, 'we have a very unhappy and confused young lady to comfort, and a funeral to arrange. Did the young man have family in the States?'

'That's what we don't know. Now that we know his name, it'll be easier to check. I'm sure the Yard is onto that. As for the funeral, that will depend on when the body is released. Certainly it won't be until they've done a complete autopsy.'

I blinked away a tear. 'I know it's foolish of me,' I said with a sniffle, 'but I hope the crash didn't damage his face. He was so handsome!'

'For Lucy's sake, I hope so, too.' Alan took my hand and silence fell.

Lucy's troubled mind didn't let her sleep for long, not nearly long enough. I wanted a nap myself, but when we heard Lucy stirring, I knew my job was to be there for her and offer what comfort I could.

'Do we have anything we can feed her?' Alan asked quietly. 'Comfort food.'

'Search me. My brain isn't working.'

'Low blood sugar,' he diagnosed, putting his head in the freezer. 'Ah. A bag full of what look like scones. When did you find time to make those?'

'I didn't. Jane must have popped them in there.'

'Microwave?'

'No, it'd make them tough. Toaster oven.'

The animals had joined us in the kitchen, well aware that it wasn't mealtime, but when the humans were preparing food for themselves, there was always a chance. Alan let Watson out and back in while I wearily put down some food for all four of them and poured myself some coffee. I hoped it might restore my ability to cope, but the general atmosphere was against it. It didn't help that the sulky rain still streamed down the windows.

Alan waited until I'd rallied a bit, and then said quietly, 'We need to talk. Before Lucy comes down.'

'Yes. I'm not looking forward to telling her.'

'What I was going to suggest, if you agree, was that we get Jane over to be with her. I don't know anyone who knows more about kids – and she still is a kid, in many ways – than Jane, or who can offer more comfort in her hard-boiled style.'

'Of course! I told you my brain wasn't working. I'll call her right now.'

Jane anticipated me. She was knocking on the door as I searched for my phone. 'Don't want to interfere,' she said in that Churchillian voice. 'Thought you might need me.'

So we were all tucked up cosily in the kitchen when we heard footsteps on the stairs, and Lucy walked into the kitchen.

She looked awful. Her eyes were swollen with tears, her nose red. She was plainly still miserable, but she was in command of herself.

'I'm sorry,' she said faintly, 'for making such a fool of myself, but—'

'Just shut up,' I said firmly. 'I'll hear no apologies for normal behaviour. You're reverting to your English roots, acting as if emotion is a social crime. You've had a terrible shock, and I wish I could send you to the bosom of your family for comfort, but you don't have one, so we'll have to do. Now wash your face at the sink – cold water – and sit down for some strong coffee.'

She obeyed, I think mostly because she wasn't up to making any decisions of her own. Alan poured coffee and heated up a few more scones, and he and Jane and I chatted about nothing while Lucy drank the coffee and crumbled a scone.

The mantel clock chimed five thirty. 'Oh,' said Lucy. 'It's maybe too late . . . I should . . . I don't know what I should do about the conference.'

'I already put in a call to the provost of the university,' said Alan. 'He's an old friend and was very understanding. He said he'd get in touch with the organizers of the conference and explain the situation.'

'Oh,' she said again, helplessly. 'I don't know what they'll want me to do.'

'Nothing,' said Jane. 'Can't work just now. We'll see to it.'

'But – but they're paying me. Quite a lot. I can't just—'

'Do as you're told!' Jane's tone of voice managed to combine authority and love. Lucy subsided.

'No way to treat my scones, either.' Jane frowned at the mess on Lucy's plate. 'Need fuel. Any more, Dorothy?'

'I'm afraid those were the last. But I can make toast and boil an egg. How would that do, Lucy?'

She shrugged, so I busied myself about making and serving that spartan meal, while Alan rambled on about the differences between the England and American cultures, and the

adjustments he and I had both had to make in our expect-
ations of each other, and Jane dug up a few funny stories
about American kids she'd had in her classroom over the
years, and Lucy managed to eat a little.

Alan looked at Jane, who nodded. 'Now, my dear,' he said,
'I'm afraid we're going to have to talk about Iain a bit.'

'Yes, of course.' She was making a real effort to appear
calm. 'I don't understand anything about it. You think . . .'
She swallowed hard. 'You think that car ran into him
deliberately, don't you?'

He didn't ask how she'd come to that conclusion. 'The
Met – sorry, the Metropolitan Police, i.e. Scotland Yard – and
I are agreed that it's a strong possibility.'

'But why? Why would someone in London . . . I mean, I
don't think he even knows anybody in London. Knew.'

Her voice shook as she changed the tense, but she blinked
back the tears.

'We have some ideas about that, Lucy, and I'm afraid
they're going to be hard for you to hear. The sad fact is that
your fiancé was not all that he seemed to be.' He gave her a
moment to absorb that, and then went on. 'You will have
gathered from the news report that Iain Campbell was not his
real name. Unfortunately, some of the other things he told
you were also untrue. His father – that is, the father of William
Gray – is long dead, never lived in North Carolina, and was
never employed by the Biltmore Company. No one by the
name of Iain Campbell ever attended any of the universities
he claimed, and so far we haven't been able to find records
of William Gray, though that search is continuing.'

Alan paused and looked at Jane. She made a gesture as of
one pulling off a bandage.

Alan took a deep breath. 'And I truly hate to have to tell
you that the ring he gave you is a replica. The gems are
excellent counterfeits, but counterfeits nonetheless.'

'You said you had it insured,' she said in a near whisper.

'And so I did. Imitation gems of that quality are rather
costly. The ring is insured for five hundred pounds.'

Lucy was silent for a long time, with Jane keeping a
close eye on her. When at last she spoke, her voice sounded

computer-generated, shorn of all emotion. 'So the whole thing was a fake, right from the start.'

Jane nodded. ''Fraid so. Looks like it.'

'So I've been a damn fool.'

I opened my mouth to deny it, but Jane silenced me with a glare. 'Like everyone else,' she said matter-of-factly. 'Proves you're human.'

'How could I be so stupid? So blind?'

I stepped in. 'He was a very good-looking young man. You tell us he had a pleasing manner and spoke well. That made him the perfect type for a con man, which, I hate to say, is almost certainly what he was. You are a very attractive young woman, and were essentially alone in a big city, with no family, few close friends. You dress nicely, carry yourself with confidence, and look . . . well, it's subscribing to a stereotype, but you look wealthy. Which you are, I gather. I imagine he spotted you as a likely mark, and when you told him what you do for a living, your fate was sealed.'

'What does my job have to do with anything?' She sounded almost belligerent, which was certainly better than limply wretched.

Alan sighed. 'I'm afraid it might have had everything to do with it. As a fundraiser, you deal with wealthy donors. You presumably have a database full of names and amounts of their donations. If he could get his hands on that information, it would be like handing him the key to Fort Knox.'

'So he could use it for his charity, you mean?'

This was probably the worst blow, even worse than the ring. 'If there is a charity,' Alan said gently. 'Given his other deceptions, there's a strong possibility that the money he raised was going to a very personal charity. It's being investigated even as we speak, but so far no such charity has been registered in the States. As, I note, is required by law for legitimate charities.'

Jane and I had watched her face grow paler with each horrifying revelation. Now it took on a greenish tinge.

'I think I'm—' She held her hand to her mouth and rushed for the stairs, making it to the bathroom, from the distressing sounds that followed, just in time.

'If you say one more word about feeling you're a nuisance, I'll . . . well, I'll think of something drastic. Meanwhile, let me tell you a little about the people you'll be meeting. Penny Brannigan is an expat like me, except she's Canadian and living in Wales. She's somewhere between your age and mine, closer to mine, but not at all stuffy. She's an artist who does lovely watercolours, but she's made her living in Llanelen running a spa. All sorts of beauty treatments, hair styling, mani- and pedicures, massage, the works. We met years ago in Wales and have been friends ever since. I know very little about her husband, because they've been married only a few weeks. I know he's a photographer, mostly wild-life, I think.'

'So it's a second marriage?'

'Not for Penny. She'd had a couple of romances that didn't work out, but when she met Colin they both knew, right off the bat. He's Canadian, too, though he travels all over the world. Or did. Now that they're married, I don't know what arrangements they plan. Anyway, she's an interesting person, and I'm sure anyone she chose for her life partner will be, too.

'So, to change the subject, what would you like to do for the rest of the time you're in England? You've been away so long, I'll bet you've forgotten a lot. How about spending a day or two in London?'

She looked me straight in the eye. 'You're trying to distract me, aren't you? Make me forget about investigating Iain's death?'

Alan leaned over and took her hand. 'In part, yes. At least we want to make sure that you understand what you might be getting into. You will be asked lots of questions, probably tomorrow, whenever the Met officers are ready.'

'"Assisting the police with their inquiries"?'

'That phrase can have several shades of meaning, as I'm sure you know. You haven't been an American all your life, and I presume you may have read a detective novel or two.'

'I always thought it meant the one who was "assisting" was the prime suspect and was going to get the third degree.'

'Not usually in England; our techniques are somewhat more

civilized. However, it can also mean exactly what it says: helping the police by supplying some facts. That's what it will be in this case. They'll want to know a lot about Iain and his work. And they'll want you to understand that the less you involve yourself, the safer you will be. I'm afraid my dear wife has, over the years, had a tendency to forget that hunting down a murderer isn't a game.'

'And my dear husband has a tendency to forget that my involvement over the years has helped to solve many tangles when the police were, as one might say, baffled.' I smiled sweetly at the two of them. 'We women look at things from a different perspective, which can sometimes be useful. However' – I put up a warning hand as Alan was about to interrupt – 'what he's panting to say is exactly what I'm going to say. Certainly your ideas and your point of view are needed and will be welcome. But do not, repeat not, express those ideas to anyone except the police and the two of us. We're old hands at keeping out of trouble—'

Alan grunted.

'—and coming out of messes with our skin intact.'

The grunt turned to a muted guffaw.

'Well, more or less, anyway. You may not have that gift. And I hope you won't take offense if I say that you're too trusting for your own good.'

'Naïve, you mean.'

'Yes, to some degree. Look, Lucy, you've spent your life among nice people, people who respected your brains and obvious abilities, and though you've had to scramble up the ladder by yourself much of the time, still, you've had enough money to make that scrambling easier than it might have been. You've never, I assume, had to deal with serious, active interference in your ambitions and goals. In short, though you'll hate me for saying so, you've led a sheltered life.'

'It hasn't been easy!' she retorted. 'I earned those degrees by the sweat of my brow, I'll have you know! And a woman trying to get a doctorate in what's still regarded as a man's field is harassed every step of the way!'

'We do know, Lucy,' said Alan mildly, his fingers tented in

his lecturing mode. 'The point is, we doubt that you've ever encountered the criminal mind, except possibly the odd mugger in Chicago. And they don't quite count. They're just opportunists, probably high on something, and wanting money to get higher yet. They're not smart enough to lay out elaborate plans to deprive someone of his money. Or his life. That takes a true criminal, and fortunately, few people from a background like yours have ever encountered such a creature.'

'What Alan is trying to say,' I said, shaking my head, 'is that you're simply too nice, and yes, too trusting. That's why you're the perfect victim for a con man. And we're very much afraid that's what Iain was.'

She sat silent, thinking. 'It all boils down,' she said at last, 'to "brains aren't enough". You've got to have street smarts, too. And plainly I don't. Right?'

It wasn't really a question.

'All right. I'll accept that. I don't like it, but you're probably right. I've spent my life concentrating on academics, living with books. The only people I've had much to do with are other academics. Believe me, they can be just as nasty as anyone else, and will stab you in the back if they get a chance, but figuratively, not literally. So my question is, what do my shortcomings have to do with finding out who killed Iain?'

'No,' said Alan in his most chief constable voice. 'That's not the question. The vital question is, given your natural concern in the matter, and the perhaps vital information you may be able to contribute, how can you be kept safe from whoever wanted Iain dead?'

TEN

She sat there, shaken. I started to move toward her, to try to offer some comfort, but she waved me off.

We'd all absorbed all the caffeine we needed, and we'd be drinking various alcoholic beverages at dinner time. Herbal tea, perhaps? I had some lemon-ginger tea that I liked, though calling it tea was like calling fizzy water champagne. I was about to offer her some when she spoke.

'You're right, both of you. I am naïve. I never really took in the idea that someone could be after me, too.'

'I'm afraid you need to take it seriously, my dear,' said Alan, the policeman still to the forefront. 'We don't know the motive for Iain's murder. It could be that it in no way involves you, but it might do. And no matter what, the killer certainly doesn't want to be found, so any way you help in the search makes you a threat to him.'

'And, in fact, to everyone involved in that search.'

'Of course. But the police have extensive training in keeping that threat at bay. Moreover, they have resources at their command that no civilian does. We – they – can call on other forces, around the county and around the world. We have vast databases. We have vast experience in this sort of thing.'

'So,' I concluded, 'not to beat a dead horse, tell us, and tell the police, everything that you think might be relevant. Everything odd, even if it doesn't seem relevant. If you remember something in the middle of the night, write it down, or wake one of us if it seems urgent. Aside from that, enjoy England as much as you can with this awful thing hanging over you.' I glanced at the clock. 'And right now, we need to stroll across the Close to the Rose and Crown.'

After the flurry of introductions, the five of us sat down to drinks. The two men had pints; the women chose soft drinks. I had one of my favourites, a G & T without the G. Peter, who is a genius bartender, makes it somehow with juniper berries, and it has almost the authentic taste while enabling me to stay awake.

Alan and I had tacitly agreed not to talk about Iain, so we chatted happily about Penny's painting and Colin's photography. His next assignment, he told us with enthusiasm, was to some of the tiger reserves in India.

'Oh, aren't they the most beautiful animals in the world? I can sort of see why people used to kill them for their fur.' I got glares. 'Oh, don't look at me that way! I'm just saying

I understand the motives, long ago when no one understood about conservation. Of course it was horrible, and even worse when they were killed just for the sake of sport. Anyway, their coats are more beautiful on the cats, with those amazing muscles moving underneath! I can't wait to see your pictures!'

'Which reminds me,' said Penny, 'do you still have your cats? They're getting on a bit in years, aren't they?'

'You wouldn't know it to look at them. They're both just as arrogant as ever, maybe even more so since we got a new kitten, a beautiful little tortoiseshell.'

Lucy, who had been rather quiet, told the story of how Mike arrived. She was a good storyteller, making everyone laugh. 'And the best part is the way Watson treats him, like a little puppy.'

'Treats her,' said Colin with a smile. 'Torties are female.'

'Not this one,' I said triumphantly. 'At least according to the vet, who ought to know. If the people who dumped him ever find out he might be very valuable indeed, they'll be sick.'

'And serves them right,' said Lucy indignantly. 'To treat a helpless little animal that way!'

'You're passionate about it, aren't you?' asked Penny. 'Do you work for an animal rescue agency in America?'

'No, I'm a fundraiser for a small liberal arts college north of Chicago. That's why I'm in Sherebury, actually, leading a conference on fundraising for small colleges – universities, I mean – all over the UK. At least, I was, before—'

She stammered to a halt and Alan took over. 'Sadly, there's been an accident. A friend of Lucy's came over from the States yesterday and was killed in a hit-and-run just outside Victoria Station. Of course she's upset, and the university has kindly excused her from further duties at the conference.'

'Oh, my, I think we read about that in *The Times*! A man named Gray?' Penny looked at Lucy with compassion.

'He used another name professionally,' said Alan with great tact. 'Iain Campbell. Scottish roots in the distant past, apparently.'

For some reason I was looking at Colin, and for a moment

I saw an odd expression cross his face, as if he was startled by something. The next instant it was gone, and I wasn't sure I hadn't imagined it. The conversation turned to the appalling increase in crime of late, and some of the reasons, COVID-caused unemployment and other economic disasters, strained social relationships, and, as Alan put it, 'Just plain nastiness'. I watched Lucy, but as far as I could tell the discussion wasn't worrying her. I steered the talk now and then, making sure it didn't stray from the general to the particular, and we got through our excellent dinner with no disasters.

Alan, after the usual polite sparring about the bill, invited Penny and Colin back to the house for a post-prandial drink, and as we strolled across the Close, Colin lagged behind and murmured, 'You've forgotten something at the table. I'll go back with you to fetch it.'

There! I knew it. Something was bothering him. I called to the others, 'I think I dropped my hankie back there. Don't wait for me. I'll catch up.'

Alan, who knew quite well that I never carried a handker-chief, preferring tissues, gave me a speculative look, and then turned back to Lucy and Penny.

Colin and I stepped inside the door of the Rose and Crown, and turned aside into one of the odd little cubbyholes so often found in England's old buildings. 'I won't waste time; we don't have much. That name, Campbell. Is the first name spelled I-a-i-n?'

'Yes.'

'Then I may know something about him, something . . . shady, at best. There isn't time to go into details, but I'll do some checking and get back to you. I'd advise Lucy to tread gently.' He reached into a pocket and pulled out his handkerchief. 'In case you need proof. It's quite clean. I'm sorry it's man-size.'

I tucked it into my purse with a nod of thanks, and we hurried home.

'You found it, then.' It wasn't a question.

I stuck my tongue out at Alan, when no one else was looking. 'Yes, thanks. It wasn't quite where I thought I'd dropped it, so it took a while. What are you all drinking?'

It was one of the less-necessary questions, a time-filler until I could think of something clever. Alan nodded his head toward everyone's sherry glasses. I smiled a yes, while trying to gesture with my eyebrows that I wanted a moment to talk to him alone.

He ignored the signal and poured a glass of sherry, handing it to me with a mouthed, *not now.*

So I had to content myself with small talk. Penny's wedding, their honeymoon in Canada, revisiting old friends and familiar places, and their settling in their lovely new apartment on the Isle of Anglesey. I was a little worried lest their obvious happiness prove too much for Lucy, but she bore up very well. A tougher little lady than she looked, apparently.

When she'd had enough, she excused herself. 'It's time I checked with the university to make sure they're really okay with my bailing out. And I thought I'd take Watson for a little walk. It was great to meet you both.'

Once she was gone, I gave a huge sigh of relief. 'All right, Colin, now you can finish what you began.'

'It isn't really worth all that drama, I suppose, the "lost handkerchief" and all. Incidentally, may I have mine back?'

I produced it. '"Merely corroborative detail, intended to give artistic verisimilitude to an otherwise bald and unconvincing narrative." Turned out it wasn't necessary.'

'Did you think I'd suspect you of an improper spot of slap-and-tickle?' asked Alan mildly.

We all giggled at the thought, though Penny tried to look annoyed.

'That was one explanation that never occurred to me,' I said. 'I'm a bit long in the tooth for that sort of thing.'

'Are not. But let Colin tell his story.' Alan refilled everyone's glass and sat back to listen.

'I have to start at the beginning. Penny may have told you that I had rather a long career in an investment firm.'

'She told me you had been an investment banker.'

'Yes, and my firm made substantial investments, all over the world. Of course we always checked them out pretty thoroughly before recommending them to our clients, and I uncovered a fair amount of dirty laundry in the process. That's why I got out of it, actually. We were making a lot of money. *I* was making a lot of money, but I didn't like the taste of it. You see, our company invested in some businesses that were fairly dodgy. One, for example, was a Scottish company that engaged in North Sea oil drilling with total disregard for animal and plant life. Perfectly legal, and lucrative, but nasty, all the same.'

He took a sip of his sherry. 'And one of their board members emeritus, named in their annual report, was one Iain Campbell.'

We considered that. 'Of course, that's roughly equivalent to John Smith here,' Alan pointed out.

'Right. But the spelling is a little less common. No, that alone is not enough to blacken his name. But I found the company so questionable in its policies that I did a little extra investigating of the board, even down to where – and how – they lived. They all lived in the UK, most of them in Scotland. Except Campbell. He lived in a place called Bloomington, Indiana.'

'Indiana University!' I exclaimed. 'That's where Lucy got her baccalaureate. When was this, Colin? That you found all this out?'

'I don't remember exactly, but several years ago. I left the firm shortly afterward.'

'And do you, Alan, remember when Lucy graduated from IU?'

'No, but we can ask her when she gets back. Why do we want to know?'

'Because I've just had a letter from a friend of mine in Indiana,' I improvised promptly, 'saying her granddaughter just finished her doctorate in music at IU, and I'm wondering if the two of them ever crossed paths.'

When the other two looked confused, Alan said calmly, 'The ability to come up with a convincing lie at a moment's notice has always been one of my wife's great strengths in an investigation.'

Penny laughed. 'I've always found it a handicap that lying doesn't come easily to me. Dorothy. You're lucky.'

Bunyard shook his head. 'I'm interested not so much in what he told you, as what you saw for yourself, how he acted, what kind of person he was.'

She shrugged helplessly. 'Again, maybe everything was a lie, his whole manner . . . Anyway, he was charming. In every way, to everybody. Of course you know he was good-looking, movie-star gorgeous. He didn't fake that; it was real. He was polite, and generous. He'd take me out to the theatre, and to dinner at places like Alinea and Topolobampo.'

Seeing Bunyard's blank expression, Lucy added, 'Okay, maybe you never heard of them, but they're famous in Chicago, and very, very expensive. I never saw the tabs, but I saw the tips he left. The waiters were always very happy.'

'That's interesting. So he seemed to have plenty of money. What sort of job did he have?'

'He's . . . he was a fundraiser, like me. He had worked originally for investment firms, but then he started a charity of his own, to help Covid victims, people who'd lost their jobs, or the family breadwinner had died, or whatever.' She paused. 'Anyway, that's what he told me. Now . . .' She trailed off.

'Lucy,' asked Alan, 'when he took you out to dinner, did he pay with cash or a credit card?'

'Always cash. Odd, now that I think about it. Almost nobody carries cash these days.'

Alan and the policemen exchanged glances.

Lucy caught them. 'I guess you think that's because his credit cards wouldn't have been in his own name.'

'It's a possibility, certainly,' said the superintendent with a grim smile. 'And we found no credit cards on his person or in his effects. Now, Miss Bowman, you mentioned his generosity. Was he in the habit of giving you expensive gifts?'

Uh-oh. We'd reached the most sensitive issue.

'Only this.' She lifted the chain from her neck, the ring dangling from it. 'Uncle Alan says it's a fake. It was supposed to be my engagement ring. I don't want it now.'

And with that she collapsed into sobs.

TWELVE

helped her up to bed and made her drink a dollop of brandy, regardless of the time of day. When I got downstairs the police were still there, talking with Alan. Unprompted, I went to the kitchen and prepared a tray with coffee and biscuits.

'I'm very sorry, Mrs Martin,' Bunyard said, 'to have caused her such distress. She was doing so well until then.'

'You couldn't have known. The ring is a very sore spot. She thought it was so lovely, just like Diana's, and when she found out it was a fake, her whole world came tumbling down around her. She trusted him, you see. She believed him, believed *in* him.' I sipped some of my coffee. 'I swear, if the man weren't already dead, I'd be very tempted . . .'

'It's a very fine fake,' said Parker. 'I'd have sworn it was real.'

'I was sure it wasn't,' said Alan, 'but I took it to an expert in London to be absolutely certain. He said it's very well done, worth all of five hundred pounds.'

'That's – what – almost seven hundred dollars? I wonder if he actually paid that much for it,' I said.

'My dear,' said Alan, 'your voice would etch glass.'

'I'm willing to bet he pulled some sort of deal to get it really cheap. And while we're on the subject, where do you suppose he got the cash he was splashing around?'

'That, of course,' said Bunyard, 'is one of the things our American colleagues would very much like to know. Our concern is his murder, but as it is very likely tied in with his financial affairs, we're cooperating closely with the Yanks. The alias – whichever name it is – isn't making things any easier.'

'You're checking both, of course.' Alan's comment was not a question.

'On both sides of the pond.' Bunyard sighed. 'It would be far easier if both names weren't so common. Iain Campbell – I ask you!'

'Isn't there an old saying, "Never trust a Campbell"?' I asked.

'Indeed,' Alan replied. 'Dating back to the Glencoe Massacre, well over three hundred years ago, when a bunch of troops led by Campbell were billeted with the MacDonalds quite peacefully for several days, and then, having enjoyed their hospitality, rose up and tried to kill them all. It's the classic example of treachery.'

'Which still apparently fits.'

Alan and the two policemen talked for a little about the possibilities for faking a passport, coming to no conclusion, and then the men left, with apologies for taking up so much of our time.

After a while I stirred and looked at the clock. Nearly lunchtime, and our breakfast had been sketchy. 'Are you hungry?' I asked Alan, without much interest.

'Not really. Unless you are.'

'No, but I suppose I'd better feed the animals.' I hadn't much interest in that, either. None of them were around.

A knock at the back door summoned them, though. Watson and Mike had been upstairs, probably guarding Lucy, but now there was a new possible threat. The kitten ran so fast after the dog that he tumbled down most of the stairs. Kittens are apparently boneless; his somersaults didn't bother him in the least.

When I went to the kitchen, the sounds also drew Sam and Emmy from wherever they'd been hiding from strangers. A human had only one reason for being in the kitchen.

It was Jane at the door, with a basket in her hand and concern on her face. 'Saw the police leave. Lucy all right?'

'Not really.' I got a couple of tins of cat food and a bag of kibble from the cupboard, while the cats twined around my legs moaning about their state of near-starvation. 'Okay, Emmy! I can do it much faster if you'll stay out of my way.' Doling out food, I continued, 'The Scotland Yard people were very kind, but when they got to the subject of gifts from Iain, Lucy took off the ring, flung it down, and collapsed in tears.' I put food on the floor and stepped away from four furry bodies. 'I put her to bed with a little brandy. That was

about half an hour ago, and I haven't seen or heard from
her since.'

Jane was already on her way upstairs. Between her and
Watson, who would return to duty as soon as he'd gobbled
his food, I decided Lucy had all the care she needed just
now and looked at the basket Jane had put on the counter.
It was full of food that smelled wonderful, though I wasn't
sure what it all was until I carefully took everything out.
There was a deep pie dish covered in mashed potatoes, and
from the mouth-watering aroma I guessed fish pie. Then
there was a fruit crumble, still warm from the oven, that
looked and smelled like a mixture of rhubarb and strawber-
ries, and to go with it a glass jar full of something that
looked like custard sauce.

Comfort food! Truly Jane was a living miracle. My appetite
returned with a vengeance.

When Jane came down again, it was with Lucy in tow. They
were chatting about something, and Lucy had washed her face.
She still looked grey and woebegone, but not desperate.

'Oh, good. Jane, I was just about to serve that marvellous
meal you brought us. I hope you'll stay and eat with us. It
looks like you made enough for a small army.'

'Happy to stay.'

'Great. Lucy, could you help me set the table for four? And
try to keep Watson out from underfoot. He's the greatest trip-
ping hazard in this house. Jane, you could pour us all some
wine.'

Keep everybody too busy to brood. Sometimes it works.

It worked for a while. We were all hungry by that time,
even Lucy. Strong emotion is at least as draining as physical
labour, and once we'd recovered a little from the ordeal, our
bodies took over and demanded nourishment. Jane's food
was the sort that slid down easily. We were all pleased that
Lucy ate at least half of what was set before her, and her face
took on a little colour. It could be that Watson, lying on her
feet, and Mike, begging for titbits, did her as much good as
the food.

When she pushed her plate away, she cleared her throat.
'You're all being very tactful, but I promise I'm not going to

'Well, it's not much, but it could lead to something. Do we have any lemonade, or orange juice, or anything?'

'Would tonic do? With or without gin?'

'That would be awesome. I'm really thirsty.'

She waited until I'd brought her the can and a glass of ice, and Alan had joined us in the parlour.

'Well, see, I was calling all the donors I could think of, the friendly ones who wouldn't mind being interrupted on a busy morning.'

'Thursday morning is busy?' Alan asked, in surprise.

'Listen, when you're a multimillionaire, every minute in the office is busy, believe me. Anyway, one guy, Fred Frankson, was really interested in what I had to say about Iain, because it turns out he'd met him once, and didn't like him.'

'I thought you said everybody liked him,' I said.

'I thought they did. But Mr Frankson said he didn't trust him. I couldn't pin him down about why, he just said he had a sense Iain was too smooth, too charming, too good to be real. But that's not the best part. The thing is, Mr Frankson had also come across William Gray!'

'But—' said Alan.

'But—' I echoed.

'Yes! I know! He – Mr Frankson – had met Iain at some fundraiser thing, and had brushed him off because he was getting bad vibes about him. But then a few days later he was coming out of his office in the Sears Tower—'

'Of course,' I said. 'Where else?'

'You got it. Anyway, he's coming out and somebody runs smack into him. Almost knocked him down. And when they'd both apologized and all that, he saw that it was Iain, and made some comment. He didn't say what.'

'I can guess,' said Alan.

'So can I. But then the guy who'd run into Mr Frankson didn't seem to recognize him. Asked his name and said he'd pay any doctor bills if he – Frankson – was hurt, and all that sort of thing. Well, then Frankson took a second look, and began to have some doubts, and asked the guy his name. Which was . . .' She paused expectantly.

'William Gray,' Alan and I said in unison.

'You get the jackpot! But Frankson was still so sure it was Iain that he invited him back into the building for coffee, just to show there were no hard feelings, or so he said. Really he wanted a chance to look the guy over.'

'And I'm betting Gray didn't take him up on it,' I said.

'Right again! Said he was in a hurry, but thanks very much for being so understanding, shook his hand, and took off.'

'Could be true,' said Alan judiciously. 'He was rushing when he ran into Frankson.'

'Sure. And pigs may fly. But there's a little more. Mr Frankson's a pretty observant guy, and just as Gray shook hands he got a good look at his face.'

'And? Noticed the broken nose, the long scar, the harelip? None of which features fit Iain Campbell?' Alan seldom ventures into sarcasm; I could tell he was getting a little tired of Lucy's dramatic narrative style.

'You're making fun of me! But no, it was a lot more subtle than that. It was the eyes. Iain's eyes were blue, practically the first thing you noticed about him. I've told you. Prince Harry eyes, really gorgeous. And this William Gray character had brown eyes, sort of muddy. That's probably why Mr Frankson got a little unsure. So what do you think of that? A different man, after all?'

'Contacts,' I said promptly. 'It isn't easy to turn brown eyes to blue, whatever the old song says.'

Lucy looked blank.

'Forget it. Before your time. But the point is that blue contacts wouldn't cover up brown eyes very well, but the other way round is easy. Don't you think, Alan?'

But Alan wasn't paying attention. He was on his phone. Since he's never rude, the conversation must be important. He nodded a couple of times, clicked off, and addressed Lucy. 'That was the Met. I called to ask about the accident victim. He had blue eyes. His passport picture shows brown eyes. They're going to send people out to search the accident scene again, for brown contact lenses.'

THIRTEEN

'So that settles that,' I said with satisfaction. 'The real man was Iain Campbell. William Gray was an alias.'

'Yes. Not that it gets us very further,' said Alan. 'We don't know when Campbell assumed the other identity, nor why, nor even how – though your idea that William Gray is dead is a reasonable path to pursue.'

'But we do know when,' said Lucy, looking excited. 'Or at least we can guess. Aunt Dorothy, if your friends in Indiana turn up records for Gray, college files, all that, we'll know that . . . or no, we won't, will we? They could be for the real William Gray, or for Iain using his name.'

'The biggest help,' Alan said, 'would be a death date for William Gray.' He thought for a moment. 'There was a birth date on that passport. It's probably the real one, because it would have been on the documents Iain "stole" to establish his new identity. That gives us a place to start. Of the thousands of William Grays in the US, there can't be more than a few hundred with that particular birth date, year and all. I don't know the statistics, but it seems reasonable.

'So.' He went into his lecturing mode. 'We have a date. Now we need a place. Here again the passport is helpful. Let's see. Oh drat, no city, just "Illinois, USA". Well, that narrows it down a bit, but not a great deal. Illinois is one of the larger states, isn't it? In population, I mean.'

Lucy and I both groaned. 'The biggest in the Midwest. Chicago used to be called the Second City, after New York, of course.'

'I think maybe it's third now,' said Lucy, 'after Los Angeles. The Chamber of Commerce isn't happy about that, let me tell you. Me, I just think Chicago has way too many people.'

'And of course Illinois has a lot of other cities: Peoria, Springfield, Champaign-Urbana . . .' I sighed.

'What I'm proposing,' said Alan, 'is that we get in touch with everyone we know who's interested in genealogy and give them all the data we have. Surely there will be a state-wide database of birth registrations.'

'Don't bet on it,' I said darkly. 'Illinois doesn't have the greatest record for efficient government. I've already asked all the genealogy freaks I know to search for obituaries. I think I'll email them again with the Illinois info, and assign each of them a few cities to search for birth records. That won't help if William Gray was born in East Podunk, population three hundred twenty-seven, but we might just hit paydirt if he was born in a city.'

'We'll hope that's the case.'

'But . . . I don't get it,' Lucy complained. 'Why do we care where William Gray was born? We're trying to find out about Iain Campbell.'

'Put that good mind of yours to work, my dear. Once we have a full record of Gray's birth, I can put my American police contacts to work, and they'll have an easy time getting his Social Security number. And then his whole life is open to us – including when and where he might have met one Iain Campbell, and when and where he died.'

'There was time when Social Security cards were clearly marked "not to be used for identification",' I said bitterly. 'Then they started to be used for everything – your driver's licence, your insurance card – you were absolutely pegged by that number. And then along came the Internet, and any illusion of privacy or security was gone.'

'True, my dear, and regrettable – but in this case, potentially very useful for us.'

'It would be even more useful,' said Lucy, 'if we could find his wallet. He must have brought it with him. For one thing, he'd have to have money. And he'd need identification for some things.'

'Did he have a debit card from his bank, do you know?' Alan asked. 'Because that would be the easiest way to get money here, from a cash point.'

'An ATM,' I translated. 'And he'd need no ID for that, whereas if he tried to trade dollars for pounds at a bank, they'd certainly want identification. Probably a passport. Which he couldn't very well use without brown eyes.'

Lucy was holding both hands to her head, as if to keep it from flying away. 'This gets more complicated and unreasonable all the time! I don't understand anything! It's like a spider web that just keeps on getting bigger and stickier.'

'"Oh, what a tangled web we weave",' I quoted irresistibly.

'And everybody else gets caught in it,' Lucy moaned.

'Now look, let's think it out.' I went into schoolteacher mode. 'There were two basic things he needed to have while he was here. Money. Identification. Since he was travelling with a false passport, he didn't want to carry his own passport or wallet any longer than he had to. Would he run the risk of bringing those things through passport control and then customs at Heathrow?'

Lucy thought about it, then shook her head. 'I don't think so. He was very cautious about risk. That's one thing that made me trust him about the investments.' Her mouth twisted, but she blinked back the tears.

'So they wouldn't be on his person anywhere. And he had no guarantee that his luggage wouldn't be searched. It doesn't often happen, but he wouldn't risk the odd chance. So that leaves only one alternative. Think about it. A secure way to move things from one place to another, without interference.'

Alan got it. 'The post.'

Lucy belongs to a generation that uses other means of communication. She looked puzzled.

'This is what I think he did. I believe he exchanged a few dollars for pounds at O'Hare, just enough to buy train tickets and pay a taxi in London, if necessary. The fee for the transaction was exorbitant, but he was wealthy. He put those pounds in his pockets. Then he put his wallet and real passport in an already prepared envelope, addressed to Iain Campbell at the Rose and Crown, and dropped it in a mailbox. He paid for express service, of course. And then he climbed on the airplane, and William Gray enjoyed a first-class ride to London.'

'He *mailed* it?' Lucy might have been suggesting that he

asked Scotty to beam it up. 'But . . . isn't that taking an awful chance?'

'It could get lost, of course. But that doesn't really happen very often. And when the sender has paid for special service, the parcel gets special attention. I'd like to bet that his little package will arrive tomorrow, or Saturday at the latest.'

'But why, why, why?' Alan had lost his patience. 'Why such an elaborate charade? What had he done that made it so important to cover his tracks? As Lucy says, the web gets stickier every time we unravel part of it.'

'We're all too tired to think straight,' I pronounced. 'I'm going to scrounge some supper and then forget about all this for the rest of the day, and go to bed early. And I don't intend to get up until I feel like it!'

Plans like that seldom work out, at least for me. At six twelve the next morning, my phone rang. I was too muzzy to read the caller ID, but I answered anyway. A call at that hour was not going to be a telemarketer.

'Oh, Dorothy, I'm so sorry to wake you, but I didn't know what to do. The postman is here with a parcel from America for Iain Campbell, who is meant to sign for it, and of course that's not possible, but I didn't want to just turn him away, because it might be important!'

'It may be very important. I'll send Alan right over. Don't let the postman leave!'

Alan was already getting dressed. 'Rose and Crown?' he asked, just to confirm.

'Mm. I'll make coffee.'

'Not for me. Greta will give me some, I'm sure, and I'll have to go straight to the police with this.'

'If it's what we think it is.'

Alan didn't even bother to answer that.

I didn't think I could get back to sleep, but for once I was too exhausted for worries to keep me awake. I was still fathoms deep when Mike landed on me.

'I'm sorry, Aunt Dorothy,' Lucy whispered. 'Mike, come here!'

Kittens learn early the basic principles of Cat, one of which is that Cats Don't Come When Called. Mike strolled up to my chin, butted it with his head, and started purring and ecstatically kneading my chest, claws fully extended.

Watson, never far away from his godchild, padded in, put his paws on the bed, and whined, asking if something was wrong.

'All right, all right, I'm awake. Sort of. Get *off*, Mike. You're shredding me.'

'I didn't mean to wake you up, honest.' Lucy sounded distraught. 'I just opened the door a crack to make sure you were okay, and Mike squeezed in, and—'

'Not to worry. What time is it?'

'About nine thirty.'

'Oh, good grief! Has Watson been out?'

'He was out when I got up an hour or so ago. I let him in and fed everybody, so they're all right. I guess Uncle Alan had to leave in a hurry?'

I fell back on my pillow, not yet ready to face the day. 'Is there coffee?' I asked peevishly.

'Coming right up. C'mon, kids.'

Watson solved the problem of Mike by picking him up and carrying him, protesting, in Lucy's wake.

Lucy returned in no time with a tray of coffee, toast, and marmalade. She closed the bedroom door firmly with one foot and looked around for a place to set the tray.

'I figured you could do without the furs for a while. Can I put this on the nightstand?'

'Here, let me clear a place.' I climbed out of bed, very nearly awake by now. 'I didn't mean to turn you into a room-service maid.'

'It's okay. You've been working your . . . um . . . posterior off for me. It's the least I could do.'

I grinned. 'Would that I could work a little more of it off! Child, you're an angel, and this coffee is straight from heaven. Have some yourself.'

When I'd drained the first cup and part of a second, I put the cup down and stretched. 'Much better. Now. I let your question hang, and you've been a doll not to pester me about it. The answer is yes, Alan left very early indeed, because

Greta called – from the pub, remember? – and Iain's parcel has arrived.'

'Oh, wow! So you were right! That's awesome!'

'Well, I don't actually know I was right. I haven't seen the thing. Greta called a little after six—'

'In the *morning*?'

'That was my reaction, too. The postman was waiting, because Iain was supposed to sign for it, and Greta didn't know what to do. So Alan went to deal with it and take it to the police. And I haven't seen him, or it, since.'

'Gosh.' She took a bite of toast. 'What do you suppose is happening?'

'I could make some guesses, but he'll be home soon to tell us.'

I showered and dressed, and when I got downstairs Alan was in the kitchen devouring toast.

'You poor dear, didn't anyone give you any breakfast?'

He held up a hand while he swallowed. 'Coffee courtesy of Greta, but nothing since. I've been busy.'

'And he wouldn't tell me a thing,' complained Lucy. 'He was waiting so you could hear it, too.'

'I'm all ears!'

'First, to give due credit, you were quite right about Iain's actions.' He paused. 'Almost.'

'Oh, don't leave me in suspense!'

'The parcel was a small box, not a bag. And along with his wallet and passport – the real one – were two other items. His chequebook . . .' Alan paused. 'And what else was missing from the list Bunyard gave us? What else should have been there, what should I have instantly known was missing if I had the brains of a flea? Think about it, both of you. What does everyone on the planet, at least everyone in his age group, always have about him?'

'Oh!' said Lucy, at the same time I slapped my head. 'His phone!'

'He actually entrusted his mobile to the mail?'

'Well-padded with bubble wrap, in a sturdy box, yes. And the Met and I, and the local police, are thanking all the electronic gods at once that he did. The amount of information we can mine from that small gadget is almost limitless. Which of course is why he didn't keep it with him for the flight. He wanted nothing that would reveal his true identity, in case something happened before he reached here.'

'And something did,' said Lucy very quietly.

FOURTEEN

We respected Lucy's grief with silence for a long moment before I decided that briskness was in order. 'All right, what we all need is a proper breakfast. No, I'll make it this time, Alan. You can make some more coffee and then sit and tell us all about the find. I suppose you had to leave everything with the police?'

'Yes, but I had a good look first, and took notes.' He measured coffee into the filter, poured water, and hit the switch, while I assembled the ingredients for French toast. 'The first thing I noted was his passport, which was of great interest even at a quick glance. Lucy, how old did you say Iain was?'

'Twenty-six. He's going to be . . . would have been twenty-seven in November.'

'Wrong. He turned thirty-two in February.'

'But – but why should he lie to me about such an unimportant thing?'

'I think I know why,' I said, beating eggs. 'He wanted you to think he had finished his graduate degree only a little while before you did. That way you wouldn't be liable to ask questions about what he'd been doing for a living recently.' I dipped slices of bread into the eggy mixture and put them in the butter sizzling in the skillet.

'There's another reason, too,' said Alan. 'He already had the William Gray identity stashed away, ready for use, and the birthdate on that passport matches the lie he told you, right down to the November birthday.'

The French toast was beginning to smell delicious. I put a

few links of my favourite sausage in another pan and turned up the heat. 'I suppose he was beginning to live inside William's skin, so he wouldn't slip up on small details. Very thorough.'

'Very.' Lucy's tone was Saharan. 'Do you know, I begin to think that's one reason he never tried to take me to bed. Pillow talk. He might have lost control, forgotten to keep up the façade. And here I thought it was just because he was a nice, respectful guy.'

'Okay, Lucy,' I said, changing the subject, 'get out some plates and silverware, and Alan, get the syrup. Everything's ready.'

I laugh at Alan's tendency to blame all bad moods on one's blood sugar level, but it's true that a good meal often improves a situation. The three of us dug into our sweet treat, which even Alan has learned to like (although he finds it very odd for breakfast) and the tension in the room eased considerably.

Alan made a pot of tea, since all of us were sated with coffee, and we retired to the parlour, along with the animals (who had stuck around for bits of sausage).

'All right, then, tell us what else you gleaned from Iain's parcel,' I demanded.

'Well, along with his date of birth, the place was also shown.'

'And? Don't make us beg!'

'Stockbridge, Scotland.'

Lucy and I both looked blank.

Alan assumed a look of astonishment. 'I wouldn't have expected you to know, Dorothy, but Lucy, you were born in the UK. Have you truly never heard of Stockbridge?'

She shook her head.

'Ah, well, it's quite interesting, you see, because it's the most affluent suburb of Edinburgh. Only the very wealthy live in Stockbridge. So, unless Iain was the son of the butler or gardener at an estate, it's likely that his father has quite a lot of money. I'm sure that, given the birthplace information, the Met is now trying to trace Iain's family.'

'Oh, dear, they probably have no idea he's dead! Poor souls, to have to hear it from the police!'

Alan made a face. 'It was one of the worst parts of my job

when I was a working policeman, notifying the family of a death. I tried always to do it in person, harrowing though it was. The survivors deserve that courtesy. The very worst ones involved children. Once—' He stopped and waved away whatever he had been going to say.

Too painful, even after all this time, I thought. I reached over and took his hand for a moment.

He cleared his throat and continued. 'His wallet contained a couple of hundred pounds, as well as some dollars tucked away in another compartment, for his return home, one assumes. Also a bank card and one credit card, Platinum Capital One, and his driving licence. Unfortunately nothing personal, no letters or anything of that kind.'

'And his chequebook?' I asked. 'You did say that was in the package?'

'Yes. The account, with Chase Bank, shows a very healthy balance. The Met will of course be in touch with them about any other accounts he might have there, savings and so on.'

'So we now know quite a lot more about him. What about the phone?'

'Off to the Met to be searched.'

Lucy spoke for the first time since we'd sat down. 'If it's an iPhone, I wish the police luck. They're very hard to hack.'

'Fortunately, no. The resident geek at the local station thought it would be easy, even for him, and the Met have superb tech resources.'

'I told him he should get an iPhone, dealing with lots of money as he does . . . did. But he was the sort of man who always knew best, even though he knew I usually knew what I was talking about.' She poured herself a cup of tea, tasted it, and grimaced.

'Cold? I'll make some more.' I got up, but she shook her head. 'I don't really need it. It was just . . . never mind.'

Watson came over and rested his head in her lap.

None of us had been paying attention to the weather, but as I looked out my beautiful, inconvenient, diamond-paned windows I saw that it was a perfect day, more like May than April. 'Let's go for a walk,' I suggested. 'We all need some exercise.'

Watson had of course perked up at the magic word. Getting on in years he might be, but a walk was still one of his favourite things. He got to his feet and went in search of his leash.

'Not me,' said Alan. 'You forget I've been on the go since the crack of dawn. I'm going to take a nap.'

'Well, before you do, make sure Mike doesn't get out. The others won't try to follow us, but Mike might, and I don't know if he's street smart yet.'

Neither the dog nor the kitten was happy about the separation, but Watson soon recovered in the sheer joy of being out in the beautiful day, with all the lovely smells to investigate.

'Do you remember the park?' I asked Lucy. 'Near the river? It's a great place for dogs and kids. Away from traffic so they can run all they want to.'

'I do, now that you mention it. Doesn't it have a pond where you can sail boats?'

'And grass to roll in, and a big field free of trees, where you can fly kites. Not on a day like this, though. March is the time for kites.'

We headed happily for the park, Watson leading the way. When we got there, I let him off the leash and he ran happily, amazingly spry for his age. He knew most of the other dogs and they all got along well, but I kept an eye open for trouble. We wandered idly, leaving our problems behind for the time being.

'How are you this gorgeous day, Dorothy?' The voice came from behind me.

'Inga! How nice to see you! And who is this?' The puppy beside her wriggled all over with the joy of being noticed.

Inga picked him up. 'This is Dog. He showed up and the kids insisted we keep him, even though we already have the two. They haven't got around to naming him yet. We've only had him a week, and they're fighting about it. Greta Jane thinks he should be Spot. She's been reading an old American children's book. The Nipper says that's silly, he doesn't have any spots, and he's going to be very large, so he should be called Rumblebuffin. *He's* been reading the Narnia books for the nth time.'

We both laughed. 'Well, I'm glad their choices are literary, anyway. Greta's book was a first-grade reader when I was a child, Dick and Jane and Spot and Puff. Ah, the memories. Lucy, you remember Inga Evans, don't you? They were at church last Sunday.'

Plainly Lucy didn't remember. Too much had happened since then. But she pretended she did, and petted the puppy. 'I can't tell what kind he is. I'm afraid I don't know a lot about dogs.'

'No recognizable breed, I'm afraid. Nigel thinks he's part Alsatian, though, so he may indeed grow to be a big boy. He eats enough for three.'

'And where are the kids?' I looked around, but didn't spot them anywhere.

'They're spending the day at the seashore with Nigel. They've been pestering us for weeks now, but the weather hasn't been great, or we didn't have time. Today Nigel finally gave in. He's just about to start a huge new project, designing a whole new accounting system for the university, so he gave himself a day off to clear his head. I don't trust this little one near the sea yet, so I stayed home to tend to him.'

I was about to make some comment about the demanding needs of puppies when Lucy spoke. 'Accounting? Is he an accountant, then?'

'No, he's a computer expert. A geek par excellence! His speciality is programming, but he can also de-bug anything, solve operating problems, pretty much anything. I don't actually understand what he's talking about most of the time, so I just nod and smile. He isn't fooled!'

'Hmm. I wonder—'

They waited, but Lucy made a throwaway gesture. 'Never mind. Just an idle thought.'

I would have pursued it, but just then Watson came padding back, plainly tired from his play session, and not too happy to see an unfamiliar puppy in his friend Inga's arms.

'Oops! Better get the old boy home.' I clipped on his leash. 'He'll get to know your new baby another time. Bye.'

I waited till we were out of the park and nearly home before I said, 'Okay, what was that about?'

'Well, see, I just thought, if Nigel's such a hotshot, he might be able to find out a lot of stuff from Iain's laptop. And then I remembered that it's back in Chicago.'

'Ah, but we have his phone, remember. And from there to his laptop is but the push of a button or two.'

'Only we *don't* have his phone. Uncle Alan had to turn it over to Scotland Yard, and who knows when they might let us have it back. If they ever do. I guess we don't actually have any legal right to his belongings.'

'Perhaps not. Probably not. But Alan is well-respected by the police hierarchy. If he proposes that he could save the Met a lot of time, and free up one of their technical experts, they'll listen. And if he further reminds them that we have, here on the spot, someone who might be able to explain any cryptic references to people, or places, or whatever, I think they'll jump at it. It's a brilliant idea, and Alan will be kicking himself for not thinking of it.'

'Ooh! Let's go home and tell him!'

'Not if he's still napping, though. Us old folks need our rest.'

'Huh! You're not old. You've just had a lot of birthdays!'

Watson, counting himself among the old folks, went straight to his basket in front of the fire. No fire on a day like this, of course, but Mike had found it a comfortable spot for a snooze. Watson nudged him aside, put a protective paw over him, and was snoring inside thirty seconds.

Alan *was* still napping, so Lucy and I busied ourselves in the kitchen, trying to come up with a light lunch from a depleted larder. I had just about decided a quick trip to Tesco was in order, when Alan's phone rang. He'd left it on the kitchen table, so I answered it, but only a moment before I heard him coming down the stairs. *Old fire-horse*, I thought to myself. *Wakes to the sound of the bell.*

'Yes, he's right here.' I handed it over. 'Superintendent Bunyard.'

I sometimes miss the old days of the landline, when I could listen in on an extension. It saved a lot of tedious repetition. But the convenience of a mobile outweighs the joy of eavesdropping. I guess.

This time the conversation was short, consisting at Alan's end of sounds of disappointment and understanding.

'Well, it seems we'll have to wait a while for information from Iain's mobile,' he said when he'd clicked off. 'They're understaffed at the Met, like everywhere else, and their two best tech people are in the midst of a complicated upgrade to their computer system. They reported that to our local guys, who said they'd rather wait and make sure the job is done well. So . . .' He shrugged.

Lucy refrained (with difficulty) from interrupting, but seeing her broad smile where he had expected despondency, Alan gave her a quizzical look and said, 'All right. Out with it.'

'It's only that I've had this marvellous idea, and now maybe it'll work. I just found out Nigel is a world-class geek. I'll bet he could unlock all the secrets of Iain's phone in nothing flat. And then we'd have access to his laptop, besides. Do you think our local police will buy it?'

Alan smacked his head. 'That's the second time in a couple of days I've overlooked the obvious. Good job I've retired, or they'd sack me. It's the ideal solution, Lucy. Quite irregular, but I'll talk them around. We all want this settled yesterday!' He picked up his phone again, and Lucy and I gleefully went back to the problem of lunch.

FIFTEEN

Alan joined us shortly. 'It's working out. Our local police are delighted. The sergeant in charge of the case at this end is going in to the Yard this afternoon to get the phone and bring it back, and then all we have to do is talk Nigel into his part.'

'He'll be over the moon, and you know it. There's nothing he likes better than a meaty job of hacking, and he doesn't get to do much now that he has a responsible job and has to stay legal. I'll call as soon as he's likely to be home from the beach.'

Alan looked around the kitchen. 'I hate to mention it, darling, but were you planning to do anything about lunch?'

'No,' I said. 'There's really nothing in the house, and Jane's off on an errand of mercy for someone else. So we're going to pick up a bite at that new pub, and then you two can help me shop for the party.'

They both looked blank.

'Tomorrow. Penny and Colin and a few others for drinks and nibbles, remember?'

'Oh.' Alan tried not to sound annoyed.

'I know you hate cocktail parties, but this one will be short, since Penny and Colin have to get to bed early. And there won't be anyone but close friends. And you can talk to Nigel about the phone. Grin and bear it, my dearest husband!'

'And we'll have all sorts of scrumptious things to eat, Uncle Alan!'

'Two against one. What chance do I have?' He bowed us out the door.

The new pub, the Dark Horse, wasn't really new. An eighteenth-century one, originally a coaching inn, had fallen into disrepair after the long-time owner died some years ago, and the new owners had spruced up the building and renamed the place without destroying the atmosphere. They had also, we discovered, hired a good cook. There was nothing fancy on the menu, but their ploughman's lunch was exceptional, with good crusty bread, lovely aged cheese, and several choices of pickle. I cautiously asked for a half pint of their home brew, and found it excellent.

Then we drove to Tesco's and came home with more than we would ever use tomorrow, but the idea of leftovers was appealing.

As we stowed the perishables, I glanced at the kitchen clock. Still too early to reach Nigel. On a lovely day, the kids would beg to stay at the beach as long as Nigel would allow it, probably until they turned blue in the still-icy water.

So I puttered in the kitchen while Lucy did some tidying up and fed the animals. It wasn't mealtime for them, but in their minds, mealtime was any time there were humans in the kitchen. Besides, some of our new purchases had tantalizing smells. So Lucy let them have scraps of Brie and Gouda, roast beef and smoked salmon, and even opened a can of smoked oysters. After that I put my foot down, but the animals were content by then to wait until Lucy was alone in the kitchen. They knew a soft touch when they saw one, and even little Mike, in the short time he'd been with us, had mastered the art of the piteous look.

I put together a batch of my favourite brownies, with chocolate chips in them, and some peanut butter cookies – standard American treats. Then finally the clock rolled around to five thirty, and I thought I'd try to call.

Inga answered. 'Yes, they've been home for a few minutes. Nigel's showering, but he'll be down in a minute or two. I gave the kids a lick and a promise and sent them up to nap. They're worn out, but so happy! Nigel gave them ice cream, which of course they smeared all over, and they really need full baths, but that can wait. Shall I have him call you?'

Nigel sounded pretty tired, too, when he called a few minutes later. 'You don't know how lucky you are, Dorothy, never having had to deal with two excited small children at the seashore!'

'I remind you that I dealt for years with thirty of them at a time on fieldtrips to places like museums. The amount of trouble a child can get into in a natural history museum . . . well, anyway, you're young. You can take it. And you're faking. You had a wonderful time, too, and you know it.'

'Okay, okay!'

'And you're going to enjoy the reason I called, too, at least I hope you are. Have you ever hacked a phone, a mobile?'

'Child's play.'

'And you can get from there to the owner's computer?'

'Dorothy, what is this about? You know I have to stay legal these days.'

'This is about helping the police with their enquiries. Stop laughing, it's the truth. You know about the death of Lucy's fiancé, of course?'

He sobered quickly. 'Yes, poor kid. Lucy, I mean. The word is that the police are treating it as murder.'

'They are, and one tool that's going to help them immensely is the man's phone.' I told him the story of how we got possession of it. 'The fact that he was so cautious about the possibility of a search implies that there are secrets there. Can you dig them out?'

'Is it an iPhone?' He sounded hopeful.

'No. I'm told they're harder to crack.'

'Yes, that would have been a real challenge. How about the computer? Mac or PC?'

'I have no idea. Lucy probably knows. Wait a minute.' She was playing with the kitten. I caught her eye and turned on the speaker. 'Nigel wants to know whether Iain's computer is a Mac or a PC.'

'PC. Only a few months old.'

'I'd like to talk to her.'

I handed it over, leaving the speaker on, but the conversation that followed might as well have been in Greek for all I understood. They were apparently discussing various features of the machine. Lucy's answers seemed to be satisfactory, for Nigel finally said, 'Right. It'll take a while, but I can do it. Probe it to the bone, open its Sesame, unmask its maze—'

'I get you. Leave no avenue unturned. Can Alan bring it to you after we have a bite to eat?'

'Any time. I can't wait!'

I sent Lucy out for some Indian take-away, and then she and I spent the evening getting ready for the party. Alan strolled into the kitchen, looked around, and said, 'I thought you said this was to be a simple get-together for friends, not a Buck House reception.'

'People must eat, you know. Do go away, dear, you're in our way.'

The truth was, I hadn't had a party for some time, and I enjoyed digging out my favourite recipes for hors d'oeuvres. With someone to help, they weren't nearly such a bother to make, and they did look festive as we filled tray after tray.

'Right,' I said finally, sinking into a kitchen chair. 'That's enough for twice as many guests as we'll have, and anyway there's no more room in the fridge. The ham balls can go in the freezer, and the tart shells. We'll finish those off tomorrow. Meanwhile, I'm more than ready to sit down with a glass of something.'

One thing about wearing yourself to a frazzle, you sleep like the dead. I didn't wake up Saturday morning until Alan brought me coffee, and even then it took a second cup before my brain was firing on all cylinders.

Lucy was already in the kitchen beating eggs and making toast. 'Scrambled okay for you?'

'Wonderful. I feel guilty, though, letting a guest do the work.'

'Hey, I'm not a guest. And you sure let me work last night!'

'True. And gratefully.' I almost said something about her making someone a fine wife someday, but bit my tongue in time. She was feeling so much better, but marriage was not a subject to discuss just now.

We polished off breakfast in a hurry and then went into high gear. Even a simple party requires a lot of work, especially the last-minute things that one forgets until almost too late. The house was reasonably clean and tidy, but where there are animals there is fur everywhere, and there's no point in cleaning it off the rugs and cushions the day before. I banished Sam and Emmy to the garden, but I didn't trust Mike not to run off, so he had to stay inside, and of course Watson wouldn't leave his adopted child. Then dusty glasses had to be run through the dishwasher, and I had to hunt up the pretty paper napkins I knew I had somewhere. I didn't have to worry too much about ice, since many of my guests were English, but Lucy and I would want some in our drinks, and my fellow ex-pats Lynn and Tom Anderson, and maybe Penny and Colin, and the white wine had to stay chilled; I filled an extra couple of trays just in case. And did we have enough tonic, and limes? And those tart shells had to be filled with the crab mixture, and, and, and . . .

I sent Lucy off to dress early, so she could play hostess if someone arrived before I got downstairs. And sure enough, the doorbell rang just as I was putting on my earrings. I hurried and got downstairs as Alan was pouring drinks for Nigel and Inga.

All of us were eager to talk to Nigel about what he might have found, but before I did more than smile at him, the doorbell rang again, and then again, and Jane came in the back way, and the party was in full swing.

There were only a dozen of us in the room, but our house is old, and the rooms small, and of course there were the animals. Sam and Emmy went upstairs to safety, but Watson, who loved parties, stuck around begging for titbits, and Mike had decided that he was safe as long as he clung to Watson's back. The pair attracted quite a lot of attention – and snacks – and of course they revelled in it.

It was a good party. Penny and Colin enjoyed themselves, and were obviously sorry that they had to leave early. 'It's a long drive, you see, and there's so much to do when we get home,' Penny apologized.

'Believe me, I understand. I'm not up to a long stretch in the car these days,' I said with a sigh. 'I think you're very brave to tackle it in one day.'

Colin moved closer to the door and spoke in a low voice. 'I'll keep in touch. India isn't as far away as it used to be, though there are places where communication is a bit tricky, no Wi-Fi or mobile towers. But I'll manage. I'm worried about the Campbell situation.'

'We are, too. But progress is being made. Would it be a terrible inconvenience if I called you at home early next week?'

They both shook their heads. 'We wish you would,' said Penny. 'Colin has some lines out, contacts he thinks may be helpful.'

'Good. And it was lovely to see you again. Drive carefully tomorrow!'

The room emptied gradually until only Nigel was left with us. 'Inga was getting anxious about the kids, so I sent her home, but I wanted to talk to you all. I've made some very interesting discoveries. The most interesting of all, and I'm sorry to have to say this, Lucy, is that Iain was a married man.'

Oh, no! Another bandage torn off without mercy. I started to move over to comfort Lucy, but she seemed to be reasonably calm.

'It's okay, Nigel. I'm not actually that surprised. It all fits, really, now that I look back. He . . . oh, I should have known he never really cared about me.'

Depressed, but not devastated, I decided.

'There's more, I'm afraid. Are you sure you want to hear this?'

'Yes. I want to know the worst.'

'He was married to a man.'

Lucy took a deep breath. Alan picked up a bottle and refilled her glass, adding a modicum of water.

'That makes even more sense. That's why he never cared much about showing affection. We kissed a few times, but it was like kissing a brother. I could tell he really didn't like it much. And when we were with other people, which didn't happen often, it was the men he wanted to talk to. I thought he was just talking business.' She took a deep draft from her glass. 'I must be the stupidest woman in America.'

'No!' I couldn't let that go by. 'It wasn't you. You were in the hands of an expert con man. At least he never got his hands on your money.'

'No fault of mine. And I think about all the other people he must have bilked! Nigel, were you able to find out anything about them?'

'Not a lot, yet. All the business files are well protected, several layers of encryption. He knew what he was doing with computers, that's for sure.'

'Oh, he was good at everything criminal!' Lucy finished her drink and put the glass down. 'I think I need to hole up for a while and try to digest all this. Night, all.'

'She'll cry herself to sleep again,' said Alan sorrowfully.

'No, I don't think so.' I shook my head firmly. 'She's a fighter, too angry to cry right now. If she sleeps at all, it'll be thanks to the bourbon. She's healing.'

'I hope so. It must be an awful blow, knowing the man you thought you loved was in love with someone else, and a man, at that.'

'I'm not sure,' I said thoughtfully. 'It means the situation had nothing to do with her, really, her attractiveness or whatever. No woman could compete. The hurt is in knowing how completely she was deceived. Nigel, have you found out anything about this guy he was married to?'

Nigel shook his head. 'Not even his name. He's a very shadowy figure.'

'Yes,' said Alan. 'The shadow in the background. Nigel, it's important that you track him down, if you possibly can. Police on both sides of the Atlantic are very anxious to have a little chat with him.'

SIXTEEN

Sunday morning. I woke with a groan. I usually greet Sunday with a smile. A day of rest. The service at my beloved Cathedral, an indulgent breakfast at Alderney's, a lazy afternoon reading and napping and going for a walk with Alan and Watson – bliss.

But not today. Alan and I had piled glasses and plates in the sink last night, too tired to do anything more. I suppose there are worse messes than the aftermath of a party, but I hope I never have to deal with them. Especially with a slight headache. Not a hangover, I told myself firmly as I tried to shower the cobwebs away. I was far too old to get hangovers, and I hadn't drunk all that much last night. I wished the church bells wouldn't chime quite so loudly.

I could have used a nice friendly animal to pet, but none of the furs came to greet me. Alan was off somewhere and hadn't brought me coffee. Feeling unloved and distinctly out of sorts, I threw on the first clothes that came to hand and grumped down to the kitchen.

Which was a scene of peace and plenty. Jane was sitting placidly with a cup of coffee, surrounded by animals whom she was feeding with bits of sausage – which she had certainly brought, as I knew there was none left in the house. Last night's dishes and leftovers were nowhere to be seen. The kitchen gleamed, and smelled blessedly of coffee and – could it be? – pancakes, and serenity.

Lucy grinned and handed me a large mug full of coffee. 'I woke up early,' she said, waving her hand around the kitchen. 'And so did Jane.'

Speechless, I just shook my head. Alan bestirred himself and put a plate of pancakes and sausage in front of me. 'There are crab tarts, if you'd rather. But whatever you prefer, you'd best get on with it if you intend to show up in church this morning.'

'Slave driver.' I tried to sound grumpy, but it's difficult with a mouth full of pancake and butter and . . . where on earth did someone find maple syrup?

After church we talked to Nigel and his family while toying with stewed tea and ignoring tired biscuits at coffee hour. 'I played around with Iain's files for a while last night,' he said quietly. 'I really do have to hand it to him. He knew almost as much about encryption as I do.'

'But not quite?' Alan had a glint in his eye.

'Not quite. Far too much to have been on the side of the angels, I fear, but I did manage to crack most of his codes and decipher almost all of his files.'

'Almost,' said Alan. 'Not the identity of the Shadow?'

'I'm close. Very, very close. I've promised the kids an outing this afternoon – Brighton, of all places – but when I get home I'll hit it again.'

'Brighton, on a beautiful, summery day like today? And they just went to the beach on Friday, anyway.' I was dubious. 'Won't the place be jammed?'

'It will. And the roads getting there will be worse. But I promised.'

'Daddy.' His son was tugging at his jacket. 'Didn't we better go now? Mummy says the pier will be heaving later.'

'Mummy's quite right. We're on our way. I'll be in touch.' And led by his eager children he was off.

'Heaving?' queried Lucy, her brow furrowed.

'Crowded, jam-packed. Everyone getting hot and sunburned

and irritable. Better them than me. Let's head for home and a lunch of leftovers and a quiet afternoon.'

Little did I know!

The afternoon started out just fine. Alan had gone to the university library to look up something for the memoir that he'd never finish but was enjoying writing. BBC 3 was playing some lovely chamber music and I was stretched out on the couch, just drifting into a nap to the soothing strains of the string quartet, when Watson galloped into the room, barking insistently. Lucy dropped the book she was reading and tried to shut him up or chase him away, but he was determined. I sat up, reluctantly. 'Be quiet, dog! You are being a pest on a nice quiet Sunday afternoon.'

He whined as if in apology, and then barked all the louder.

'What *is* it, Watson? Is something wrong?'

He edged toward the kitchen and then looked around, as if wanting me to follow him.

'Maybe one of the cats has invaded the pantry,' said Lucy. 'I'll go see.'

The noise continued, growing ever more frantic. Something *was* wrong. He never acted like that. I went to the kitchen door.

I could see nothing amiss. Watson was standing at the back door, pleading for us to open it. I looked around to see if little Mike was going to try to run out, but didn't spot him, so I nodded to Lucy, who opened it and almost got bowled over as Watson pushed past her.

We followed, of course. This was such unusual behaviour for our staid old dog, I was somewhat alarmed. Did he think there was a threat out there? Someone trying to break into the house perhaps?

But he didn't rush off, barking to alarm an enemy. He stopped just outside the door, looked around, and then put his nose to the ground.

'What on earth? He isn't looking for Alan, surely.'

Lucy was quicker than I. 'Mike! Where's Mike? I haven't seen him since lunch.'

'Come to think of it, neither have I. He's always with his big buddy. Do you suppose he got out somehow?'

Watson had begun to whine dismally. He came and stood beside me, giving me one of those pleading, heartbreaking looks. *You're the human. You can do anything. Help!* 'Oh, sweetheart, I would if I could, but I don't know where he is, either.'

'We have to go look for him. Or maybe Jane—'

'She's away for the afternoon. We'll go out with Watson. I'll get his leash. And leave a note for Alan.'

'Shouldn't we call him? Mike might have jumped in the car.'

'He's in a library. He'll have muted his phone. Anyway he'd have called to tell us, knowing we'd worry. I'll be right back.'

So we set out, Watson stopping every now and then to sniff. He wasn't bothering to mark his territory, though. This was a serious search. He had to find his baby!

While Watson sniffed under bushes and at the base of trees, Lucy and I called and peered at the tops of those trees. It was still only the end of April, even if it did feel like summer, and the foliage was young and sparse. There was no kitten in any tree. We checked behind and in rubbish bins. We knocked on doors; obliging neighbours peered into garden sheds where he might have gotten trapped. No kitten.

I finally sat down on someone's front steps, worn out. Watson, in canine terms at least as old as I, was tired, too, and hot. He lay at my feet panting, now and then whining.

'I know, old boy. I'm worried, too, but I don't know where else to look.'

'I think we should call the police,' said Lucy.

'Maybe the RSPCA,' I suggested. 'It's more in their line. I'm just afraid—' I couldn't finish.

Watson, perhaps troubled by my despondent tone, sat up and barked. Then his ears stood up, he barked again, and tore the leash out of my hand as he dashed off.

We had reached the High Street, with its traffic. Cars were travelling fast. Lucy rushed after Watson while I called and scolded. I was terrified, but couldn't move fast enough to catch him.

He squeezed between two parked cars and then stopped. A

driver had seen him and screeched to a halt, but the dog wasn't interested in crossing the street. He was trying to wriggle under the parked car, whining loudly.

But not so loudly that we couldn't hear the answering mews.

Mike was unharmed, but trembling with fear. Lucy got him out, with some difficulty, from the wheel well where he was cowering, and carried him home, Watson supervising our every move.

The kitten was coated with mud and oil and unidentifiable debris. He had to have a bath; we couldn't have him and Watson licking all that crud. Mike was not happy about the bathing process. It took Lucy and me both to hold him still and make sure he didn't get soap in his eyes, and we did not escape unscathed. If you have never tried to restrain an angry, wet, slippery kitten, I don't recommend the exercise. We were of course bigger than Mike, and stronger, but he had the more effective weapons. We had prudently closed the bathroom door, not only so Mike couldn't escape, but so Watson couldn't get in. He was convinced we were trying to murder his baby, and his angry complaints overrode Mike's. The other two cats were eager to join in the fun, so that when Alan came home the house sounded like a riot at the zoo.

We were by that time almost done with the chore, having reached the drying off stage. The kitten didn't appreciate that any more than the preceding process, so when Alan braved Watson's demonstrations and opened the door a crack, Mike, still half-soaked, took a flying leap from the sink and escaped.

Eventually peace was restored. Watson captured Mike and lay down with the kitten held firmly between his paws. Mike licked and licked and licked until he got all the objectionable smell of soap off his fur, and then went to sleep, exhausted. Watson grudgingly allowed me to examine him for hidden injuries, but there appeared to be none.

Only then did Lucy and I collapse with well-earned liba-tions. Alan let us get half our drinks into us before plaintively asking for an explanation. I nodded at Lucy; she tended to be less verbose than I.

'Mike disappeared. Watson wouldn't leave us alone till we found him. He was covered in gunk, so we had to give him a bath. He didn't like it.'

'And that's the *Cliff Notes* version,' I said, forgetting that Alan had probably never heard of *Cliff Notes*. 'Finding that little nuisance took us most of the afternoon. I have no idea how he got way over at the end of the High Street. He'd hidden under a car, up in the wheel well, and I don't suppose we'd ever have spotted him without Watson.'

The dog opened his eyes at the sound of his name, curled his paws protectively around Mike, and went back to sleep again.

'I've never known a dog to love a cat so much.' Alan took a sip of his own drink.

'I'm not sure Watson knows Mike's a cat. Maybe he never got to be daddy to any puppies, so this is his first chance. Anyway, it's sweet.' I picked up my empty glass and put it down again.

'Another?' Alan asked lazily.

'Not just now. I need to be doing something about dinner.' I didn't move.

'I'll put something together, Aunt Dorothy,' said Lucy. She didn't move, either.

'We'll figure it out, when we get hungry,' said Alan. 'What I can't figure out is what made Mike take it into his tiny head to go so far away.'

'Alan, he was really scared when we found him. He wouldn't come out from his hiding place, not even for Watson. Lucy had to crawl under the car and detach him, claw by claw, and he trembled all the way home. Something had frightened him badly.'

'Hmm. And he's a pretty self-confident little thing. Of course, he's almost never out alone.'

'Right. Watson's always there to keep an eye on him. But suppose he slipped out when you left for the library, and then found himself lost.'

'But why would he roam so far? He's never been out of our back garden, has he?'

'Once,' said Lucy, sounding grim. 'After those awful

people dumped him. I think they found out, somehow, that he was worth a lot of money. It was probably that story in the paper.'

The local paper had run a filler about the valuable cat that got dumped. I'd taken little notice. In a place the size of Sherebury, almost anything counts as news.

'So they knew where to find him, and came back to get him. And then he got away from them, and ran as fast as he could, and *then* he was lost, and terrified.'

I smacked the arm of my chair. 'Lucy, that makes a lot of sense. I'll bet you're right. And how frustrating that we have no idea who these awful people are. Well, anyway, thanks to Watson we have him back, and pretty soon he'll forget all about the kidnapping—'

'And the bath,' put in Alan with a chuckle.

'—and the bath, and be a happy kitten again. It'll take longer for Lucy and me to forget about the bath, though!' I studied my hands and arms, wondering if any of the scratches were deep enough to warrant first-aid.

There was a tap at the back door, and Jane's voice called out, 'Anybody home?'

She had brought us a big pan of cauliflower and cheese, along with a fresh green salad and chunks of fresh pineapple and kiwi in a big bowl. 'Precious little local fruit this early. Stuff from Spain isn't bad.'

'Jane, you've come to our rescue! We're getting sort of tired of leftover party food.'

'Reckoned you might be.'

'You'll stay and eat with us, of course. Because we would a tale unfold!'

SEVENTEEN

Jane was, of course, indignant about Mike. 'Helpless kitten!' she said. 'Should be horsewhipped.'

She meant the kidnappers, of course, not the kitten.

Lucy and I looked at our arms and then at each other, but said nothing.

Jane noticed, of course. 'Helpless against brute force,' she said. 'Like to think they're scratched even worse.'

'You do realize,' said Alan moderately, 'we're speculating here. Mike could have been frightened by almost anything, and run away.'

'Not easily scared, that one,' said Jane, and we accepted her pronouncement. She knew even more about animals than we did. 'Scratched John's nose when he ran at him.'

John, full name John Bull, was Jane's largest bulldog, weighing at least fifty times Mike's tiny bulk.

'He's a scrapper, all right,' said Lucy, looking over at the tiny bundle of fur sleeping peacefully with his protector. 'You'd never think it to look at him now, but he can defend himself pretty well. And he would have had reason to be terrified of the people who took him, if they really are the ones who dumped him in the first place.'

'Terrified, and or furious. And I don't think he would have run so far, if he had just been scared. I told you, Alan, he was way over on the High Street, almost as far as the Indian restaurant. Way out of his comfort zone. No, I was convinced he was taken there, and somehow managed to get away.'

'And I hope those awful people get infections from the cat scratches,' said Lucy vindictively. 'Maybe he even bit them, and they'll lose an arm.'

Over our heads, the cathedral bells began to ring a short peal to round off the joys of Sunday. 'A reminder to be charitable,' said Alan piously.

'Hah!' was Jane's comment. '"God shall crush the heads of his enemies."'

We looked at her, speechless.

'Psalm sixty-eight,' she added.

'Oh,' I said idiotically. 'Oh, yes. I see.'

After a somewhat lengthy pause, Alan offered to help clear the table. Jane left, and we cleaned up almost silently.

Monday morning. Gloomy, drizzly, chilly. The kind of day one greets with a snarl, before burrowing back under the covers.

The animals, however, had other ideas. They were hungry. They wanted out, or thought they did. For Watson it was a necessity. As none of the other humans seemed to be stirring, I dragged myself out of bed and down to the kitchen.

The cats accompanied Watson to the back door, and then stared at me accusingly when he ran out. 'I can't help it. I didn't make it rain, and I can't make it stop.'

Sam's comment was loud and plainly profane, but all the cats responded to the promising food noises and, I assumed, forgave me for the weather. I tried to catch Watson with a towel when he came in, but he eluded me and showered us all with a vigorous shake before settling down to his own food.

'You know, there's no law that I *have* to have pets.' I grumbled my shivery way back to bed, and closed the bedroom door.

It wasn't my day. Just as I'd got nice and warm again, and sleep was claiming me, my phone rang. Why on earth had I put it on the bedside table?

I'm one of those people who can't ignore a phone, so I picked it up to squint at the caller ID.

Nigel.

Nigel! I answered as fast as I could, but too late. The call had gone to voicemail.

Alan was stirring by now. I said, 'Coffee, dear, if you love me.' I put on my glasses, and called Nigel back.

'Sorry,' I said when he answered. 'Slow on the uptake this morning. Do you have news?'

'Do I! Alan is going to love this! I have the name and – get this – the email address of Iain's husband! Iain was a very careful and clever chap, encrypted everything, but I'm a clever chap, too!'

'And I'm sure everything you did was absolutely legal,' I said.

Alan, who was listening while he dressed, made a sceptical noise.

'Of course. Would I ever do anything illegal?'

'Well . . . hardly ever.' I sang it, and Alan chuckled as he went out the door in pursuit of coffee.

I asked Nigel to defer the rest of his revelations until we'd had some breakfast and enough coffee to respond intelligently. So we all gathered in the parlour a little later, and Alan called Nigel. 'All right, Einstein, what do you have for us? Never forgetting that I am still an officer of the law.'

'You got me, guv, it's a fair cop. Except I do, you know, have official permission to employ all my skills in the performance of my duties for the university.'

'And I'm sure you'll find a way to fit recent activities into the scope of that permission.'

'Oh, stop it, you two!' I said in exasperation. 'You both know perfectly well that Nigel isn't going to get in trouble for this, unless the guy in America decides to sue him, and we know very good lawyers. So tell us what you've learned. I can't wait!'

'Alan, I'll email all this to you, so you can share as much of it as you think best with the authorities here and in the Met. But briefly, the man's name is Robert Brinton. I even have a mailing address for him, in Boston, but it's from an old email, so I don't know if he still lives there.

'The important thing, though, is the content of the emails. They were encrypted, but even decoded, the conversations consist mostly of hints and innuendo. These guys were security freaks! But there are clear indications of highly illegal dealings, mostly financial. I'm sorry, Lucy!'

'Don't be. I won't kill the messenger. In fact, I'm beginning to realize that I felt something was wrong even weeks ago. In the immortal words of Harold Hill, I closed my eyes to a situation I did not wish to acknowledge.'

'Musical comedy character,' I said to the two baffled Englishmen. '*The Music Man*. I'll tell you later. Go on, Nigel.'

'Well, I don't know how much any of you know about high finance.'

'Nothing,' I said.

'Not as much as I should,' said Alan.

'Actually, quite a lot,' said Lucy almost apologetically. 'I have to, in my job.'

'So you know about insider trading.'

'Yes, of course. Trading stocks and securities based on

information not available to the public. Unfair, of course, and very illegal.'

'Indeed. What you may not know, though, is that the laws against it are much more stringent in America than here in the UK. I learned that from an American friend whose father deals in securities. Long story. The point is that Iain Campbell apparently didn't know that either, and was engaged in just that sort of dealing, with the help of his friend/lover/husband, Robert Brinton.

'Now, as I've said, the emails are deliberately non-specific. However, if I can pick up the hints, I'm sure people who really know what they're doing, law-enforcement people who are familiar with this sort of thing, can find out much more.'

'And there's one more thing,' said Alan grimly. 'I presume, Lucy, that in the US as in the UK, spouses cannot be compelled to testify against each other.'

'I know that,' I interrupted. 'I've read all too many mysteries where the only witness against some low life was his wife, and they couldn't bring her into court.'

'Oh!' said Lucy. 'Are you saying that's why Iain married this guy? Because they were involved in crime together, but if they were married, neither could testify against the other?'

'I'm saying it's a possibility. Though I'd have to check, or have someone check, whether that law applies to same-sex marriages.'

'I'm pretty sure it does, Uncle Alan. I know a few gay couples, and I think the law that permitted them to marry made their marriages legally equal to conventional ones. I'm not sure, though.'

'It should be easy enough to find out.' Alan made a note. 'If so, it could be enlightening to know exactly when their marriage took place. And that, again, ought to be easy enough. I can get that even through conventional channels, Nigel!'

'But I can get it quicker, and I don't even have to hack anything much. No fun at all.'

'It's a good thing, Nigel,' I proclaimed in my schoolteacher manner, 'that you decided to straighten out and fly right. You would have made a truly frightening cybercriminal!'

'It's still an option. When the kids get a little older and need to go to expensive schools—'

'You'll remember that you have a senior policeman breathing down your neck,' said Alan firmly.

'And a bit of a past,' I added. 'But you will let us know if you garner any more interesting titbits, right?'

'Not if. When.' Nigel spoke with the assurance of one who has perfect confidence in his own abilities. Which, I thought, was well justified.

Nigel ended the call, and the three of us sat looking a little blank. 'So what's next?' I asked, with a grimace. I was not feeling hopeful.

'Next,' said Lucy, springing to her feet, 'is more coffee.'

'Was I ever that young?' I said as she scurried into the kitchen.

'You still are,' lied my husband, 'when you're not discouraged and out of sorts. You're the youngest woman of your age I know.'

'Hah!'

'As for what's next, Nigel spelled it out for us, my dear. As soon as he sends us his report, I'll forward it to the Met. Their financial geniuses will work out exactly what Campbell and Brinton were up to.'

'And locate Brinton's current address.'

'That, too. So you see, all is far from lost. We're making progress.'

'But so slowly! I want answers now.'

'You'd never make a policeman, Aunt Dorothy.' Lucy came back in the room and handed me a mug of coffee. 'Sugar and cream, right?'

I tasted the coffee. 'Perfect. And I would too make a good policeman. Woman.'

'No, you wouldn't. Detective, yes. But the police have to spend ages on a case, patiently digging up little bits of information. Am I right, Uncle Alan? There's never an answer "right now".'

'Quite right. And most of those little bits of information turn out to be absolutely useless in the end. What Nigel's unearthed for us is a big piece, not a little one, and will certainly lead us to Campbell's crimes.'

'But we don't absolutely know that he was killed because of his crimes.' I was in a contrary mood.

'No. But don't forget the Law of Interconnected Monkey Business.'

So we had to explain to Lucy the theory formed by one of the wonderful characters created by mystery writer Aaron Elkins, that when a lot of dicey stuff was centred around a particular person and/or location, eventually everything will turn out to be connected.

'Hmm. Works out in fiction, maybe,' said Lucy. 'Because the author manipulates it that way. How about real life, Uncle Alan?'

He waggled his hand. 'About half the time, I'd say. As I say, much of the information that accrues around a case has nothing to do with it. Sometimes because the ever-helpful public supplies us with red herrings and dead ends, and we have to follow them up, just in case. Sometimes, especially when we're dealing with career criminals, one man will be involved in two or three fiddles at once, unconnected with each other.'

'Makes life interesting, doesn't it?' Lucy said with a grin.

I had sunk into the couch cushions. Now I sat up and looked closely at Lucy. 'You're feeling a lot better. I just noticed.'

'Actually, I am. I've stopped thinking about all this as my personal disaster. It isn't really that, anyway. The thing with Iain was never real. This has been kind of a tough way to figure that out, but I'm utterly cured of him. He was a sleaze and I'm well rid of him.'

'Amen,' said Alan and I together.

'But.' She held up an index finger. 'Even a sleaze doesn't deserve to be murdered. And the thing is, when we catch the guy who did it, maybe there'll be some way to repay the other people he conned. I'm all for justice.' She paused. 'Besides, when I start thinking about it as a maze to run or a puzzle to solve, it makes me feel like Nancy Drew. It's kind of fun, you know?'

Alan's phone rang. 'Nigel,' he said, putting the call on speaker.

'I told you I could find it,' said Nigel complacently. 'Brinton's full name, address, date and place of birth, Social

Security number, date and place of marriage. Do I get the gold cup?'

Alan groaned. 'As long as you don't tell me how you found all that.'

'A good hacker never divulges his methods. Actually, I just made a few phone calls. I'll email you all the info, but I know you're most interested in the date of marriage. He and Campbell were married in a Chicago courthouse, by a judge . . .' He paused.

'Okay, we'll play your game,' I said with a sigh. 'When?'

Nigel chuckled. 'Three weeks ago.'

EIGHTEEN

Alan and I turned to Lucy. Alan was the one who asked. 'Lucy, did something happen in your relationship about that time?'

There was fire in her eye, and she bit off her words. 'The bastard proposed to me!'

Alan was just as angry. 'He proposed marriage to you when he had just married, or was about to marry, someone else. I think your epithet is accurate.'

'Right,' I said. 'But let's think about it a little. Here we have a definite example of interconnected monkey business. The question is, did one action precipitate the other, or were both touched off by something else? Lucy, think back. Did something happen to upset Campbell about then?'

I became aware that I, like Alan, had abandoned the friendly use of the first name.

Lucy was staring into space. 'Three weeks ago. It seems like years. Let's see. Iain had been out of town for a couple of weeks. He *told* me he was talking to potential donors to his charity, and also to various agencies for lists of people who might want to apply for help. He called me every day, and told me some pitiful stories. He should have tried to earn a living writing romances! He made up some real tear-jerkers.

I thought, even at the time, that they were almost too awful to be true.'

'Where exactly did he say he was?' asked Nigel.

'All over southern Indiana. Bloomington, Nashville, Columbus, even down to Hillsburg and Madison.'

The names were all familiar to me, of course. I'd grown up in Hillsburg, taught there, married there . . . I thought for a moment. 'Back in my day, there wasn't a great deal of wealth in that part of the state. Poverty, yes, the worst kind of rural poverty. I suppose things have changed.'

'Dorothy, my dear,' Alan reminded me, 'only the wealth would be of interest to Campbell. The question of poverty wouldn't have mattered. Even if he was where he said he was, he wasn't raising money for charity.'

'Oh yes, he was. His own. They do say charity begins at home.' Lucy's face was set, her voice hard.

I began to worry about Lucy's anger. It was justified, but too much acid damages the container. Time for another direction. 'And how did he act when he got back? Did you get the impression the trip had been successful?'

'No, as a matter of fact. Now you mention it, I remember that he was really down in the mouth. I didn't ask him about it – he got touchy when I asked about his business – but he started talking about needing someone to cheer him up, someone to soothe him and keep him productive.'

'And that's when he proposed.'

'Yes. I even teased him about it. Asked him if he was looking for a wife or a nanny.'

'Or a scapegoat,' put in Nigel. 'Look, I've got to go. There's some stuff I have to get on with. I'm just sending all this info to you, Alan.'

'And we can't thank you enough. I mean that, Nigel. If I can return the favour somehow—'

Nigel laughed. 'I'll remember that when I get my next speeding ticket. Bye.'

'Well,' I said, after a pause. 'We need to start working on a plausible scenario. But first, more coffee.'

'No,' said Alan firmly. 'First, look at the clock. It's lunch-time, and we had a very sketchy breakfast.'

I'd actually forgotten that, but the reminder prompted an immediate growl from my stomach. 'Oh, my, yes. Brain food. I wonder if Jane's provided some more bounty.'

'Give her a break, Aunt Dorothy! She's been running a one-woman catering service for us. I'm sure we can come up with something.'

Between us we unearthed a lasagne I'd forgotten about, tucked in the back of the freezer. It didn't take too long to defrost it, just long enough to throw together a salad and make some quick garlic bread.

'This,' I said as we sat down at the table, 'is not my idea of a May luncheon, but I thought it might do for a day straight out of March.'

None of us ate a lot. The food was good, but we didn't want to eat ourselves into a stupor, so easy to do with a heavy load of carbs. We drank water rather than wine, for the same reason, and when we went back to the parlour with fresh coffee, Alan built up the fire to only a modest size. Cosy comfort was not what we needed just now.

'All right,' I began in my schoolteacher voice. 'I have an agenda. We need to try to figure out what Campbell was doing while he was roaming around southern Indiana. I think we can take it as given that he was up to no good, but do we have any ideas about what, exactly?'

'Oh, we can come up with lots of ideas,' said Lucy, scowling. 'The trouble is, how are we going to know if any of them are true?'

'That's where we're going to need to cooperate with the American police forces,' said Alan. 'Dorothy, you and I know several officers in Hillsburg, and that's close enough to Bloomington that I'm sure there will be connections, people who know people, and so on. If we can map out a set of assumptions that seem to make sense, then we can present our ideas to our American cousins and see what they can do to verify any of them. Or, of course, to prove us wrong.'

'Okay.' Lucy sat up, looking suddenly bright-eyed and bushy-tailed. 'And if he was doing what I think he was doing, I know people who can help, too. People in finance.

Don't forget we were supposedly in the same business, only mine was – is – honest.'

'Then let's start with your ideas.' I picked up my notebook from the end table.

'There are so many things all mixed up together that I don't even really know *where* to start. But first, I think he's going to be pretty hard to trace, what he was doing, I mean, because I think he was probably William Gray at the time.'

I frowned. 'How do you work that out?'

'We decided that he had set up that identity long ago, to step into when he needed to disappear for a while. Now suppose the SEC or somebody had found out something wonky about Iain Campbell's financial dealings. That would be an ideal reason for him to switch identities.'

'Wait, though.' I ran my fingers through my hair. 'Had he been dealing all this time as Iain Campbell? Why aren't there records of all this in that name?'

'Because the louse was a computer genius! Nigel said so, you know. I'll bet he could make things appear and disappear with the flick of a mouse. Your contacts finally found records of William Gray's education and stuff, right? A whole biography of someone who never existed.'

I shivered. 'That's . . . frightening.'

'No more so,' said Alan, 'than the compromising photographs one often sees of two people who never met, in real life. Technology has almost abolished the concept of truth.'

'So you're saying, Lucy, that a computer search for either Gray or Campbell is going to be useless? Where does that leave us? Up a creek, it seems to me.'

'Not if Nigel does the searching,' Lucy asserted. 'He's proved that he knows his way around the net. There are only so many ways to hide stuff, and really very few ways to delete anything permanently. A file on your own hard drive, yes, probably. You can take the hard drive out and destroy it, and the file's really gone. But that's only if you've never sent it to anybody, or filed it in the cloud, or been hacked. It's scary, all right. You need to understand that nothing you do on a computer is private. And as for a smart phone, fugeddaboudit!'

That broke me up. Her accent, English heavily overlaid with American and now faux Brooklyn, was too much.

'All right, ladies,' said Alan, pounding an imaginary gavel. 'Order in the court. Do we have any idea of when Campbell became Gray?'

'We could find out from Colin when there were still records of Campbell,' Lucy offered. 'Because he found him, remember, when he was looking up board members of that iffy company. We know it was after he moved to America.'

'That's a start. Dorothy, remind me. Are Colin and Penny still in the UK, or have they already headed off to tiger territory?'

'Let's see. They went home yesterday, and said they had to leave for India three days later. So yes, they should be in Anglesey now.'

'And you have their mobile number, because Penny called you a few days ago. So call, or text, and ask Colin about that date. Then, if you will, start checking your Indiana sources for anyone who might have heard anything about Campbell in late March or early April, and I'll do the same with the Hillsburg police. We're looking for Campbell and/or Gray, remember.'

Colin and Penny were frantically busy packing and making final arrangements for their journey, but Colin came to the phone readily and gave me an approximate date. 'It would have been five or six years ago. I can look it up for sure when life is settled again, but right now all my journals and notes are packed who-knows-where.'

'Don't worry, this is close enough. I'm so sorry to bother you, and I wish you a wonderful trip. Let us know your address when you have one!'

He promised, and I had barely ended the call when my phone rang.

'Jane here. Someone Lucy should meet. Now?'

'Sure.' I had no idea what Jane was up to, but if she thought Lucy should meet this person, it was fine with me.

I looked at my phone as she disconnected. Good grief, the afternoon had flown, and it was nearly teatime. I got up (with some difficulty, having sat too long) and said, 'Jane's coming over, with someone she wants Lucy to meet. I'm going to make tea.'

There wasn't a thing in the house in the way of tea pastries, but I was pretty sure Jane would bring something.

She did, coming in the kitchen door with a large plate of scones, and behind her a very pretty young woman. 'You don't know me, Mrs Martin, but I've heard a lot about you, and I'm happy to meet you.'

She didn't get a chance to say more. Lucy came flying into the kitchen. 'Carrie? Carrie! It can't be you!' And then they were crying and hugging and talking so fast neither could understand the other.

'Old school friends,' Jane explained. 'Give them time.'

The kettle boiled. I had made the tea, warmed the scones, prepared a tray, and taken it all into the parlour before the two girls calmed down.

'All right, ladies, sit yourselves down and let me pour you some tea. I can see you're delighted to see each other again, but the tea won't improve by stewing. I haven't even learned your name, my dear. Milk or lemon? Sugar?'

'Oh, sorry, sorry! I'm Caroline Rhodes, and Lucy and I went to school together donkey's years ago. Well, actually, Caroline Carlson, but I was Rhodes back then. I don't live in Sherebury anymore, but darling Miss Langland rang me up, thought I'd like to see Lucy again.'

So we had our tea, with the girls talking nineteen to the dozen, full of 'do you remember' and 'whatever happened to', interrupting, laughing, making very little sense. Alan gave up trying to follow the conversation and repaired to his study, probably to email his American friends. I got a little information from Jane.

'Friends when they were babies. Lucy moved, different school. Caroline went off the track.'

'What do you mean, off the track?'

'In my school by then. Smart, but wild. Bad choices.'

The two girls had stopped talking for an instant, and Caroline heard Jane. 'Is Miss Langland telling you the story of my misspent youth? It's all quite true.' She grinned at her friend. 'When Miss Priss wasn't around as a restraining influence, I went off the deep end. Boys, drink, even tried drugs once or twice. Mum was frantic, poor dear. She and Lucy's mum were friends, so they wrote to each other. Mum was sensible enough not to lecture me about how well you were doing, old dear.' Lucy stuck her tongue out, and they both laughed. 'She did pass along your news now and again, honours and all that, and I resented you at the same time as wishing I could be like that.'

'And I,' said Lucy, 'envied your freedom and the fun you were having. But I'm not like you. I'm . . . I guess driven is the word. I had to study, had to get into the university I wanted, *had to* do well.' She looked apologetically at Caroline.

'We were never alike,' Caroline agreed. 'But we made a good pair when we were kids. You kept me out of trouble, most of the time, and I gingered you up. But then you left, and I went right round the twist. And you never wrote, or called, or anything, just disappeared.'

Lucy looked at her hands. 'That was partly Mum. She didn't really approve of you, you know. I guess she thought you were a bad influence.'

'I was,' said Caroline, also looking down. 'I don't know how much you knew, how much your mother told you, but let's just say I was headed straight for disaster when your parents died. Mum wrote to you, and then you wrote to me, and then we were friends again, just like before. Lucy, you know I'm not the type to go all sentimental, but it's quite true that you saved my life.'

'Oh, don't be silly!'

'I'm not. I thought I was in love with this boy at my school. He was everything my family hated. Miss Langland can tell you.'

Jane nodded emphatically. 'Drugs, theft, a rotter. In prison now.'

'We were going to get married. I told him we'd better get on with it, because I thought—'

She patted her stomach, and Lucy nodded calmly. 'But you weren't.'

'No, thank God. Anyway, the louse said he'd never marry me and if I was in the club I'd better get rid of it. Well, that did it. That and your letter. You sounded so nice and normal. Sad, of course, because your parents were gone, but you had big plans. I had nothing.'

'Brains,' said Jane firmly. 'Guts. Just needed to grow up.'

'Anyway, that's the story of my life. Condensed. I finished school, went to university, met a wonderful man, married him, and now have a very naughty two-year-old. If you hadn't straightened me out, I'd probably be in prison, too. Or dead, if I'd kept up with the coke.' She put down her teacup. 'Of course, if you'd stayed here, I wouldn't have got into all that mess to begin with.'

'I wouldn't be too sure of that, Carrie. I got into a pretty big mess with a lying cheat myself, as you probably know.'

'That's why Miss Langland wrote to me.'

'Thought you'd like to see each other again,' said Jane, daring us to imagine any more complicated motive. She glared at me and held up her cup. 'Any more tea?'

NINETEEN

I stood. 'I'll make some more. Or does anyone want something more interesting?'

Alan stepped into the room, having heard that the babble had died down. 'If I'm included in "anyone", I'm open to suggestions.'

'Bourbon? Scotch? Sherry? The sun's well over the yardarm, and it's time for a bourbon for me.'

'Me, too,' said Lucy.

'Ah, you've picked up American ways!' accused Caroline. 'I'd love some sherry.'

I knew Alan and Jane preferred Scotch, or whisky as they'd call it, so I poured the drinks and raised my glass in a toast. 'To reunited friends.'

The talk became general. I carefully steered it that way,

thinking we'd had enough for the time being of old, unhappy, far off things. Alan built up the fire. The animals, deciding that the new person was harmless, returned and distributed themselves among the laps or, in Watson's case, feet. (We finally convinced him, a couple of years ago, that he was *not* a lap dog.) Carrie told us about her husband and their little boy and showed us pictures.

When I was beginning to worry about the question of supper, Jane stood and settled the matter. 'Time to be off,' she said brusquely.

'Oh, but there's lots more to talk about!' cried Lucy.

'Not tonight, though.' Caroline took her hand. 'I've stayed too long as it is. My demanding son will be driving his father mad by now. Ryan's quite good with him, actually, but the little monster wants *me* to feed him and put him to bed, and when he's annoyed, he lets the world know about it.'

Alan, who no longer had to deal with screaming children, said in a patronizing tone, 'You must let him know who's boss.'

'Oh, he has no doubt about that. That's the trouble.'

'But Carrie, you can't just go away!' Lucy wailed.

'Darling, I live twenty minutes away, this side of Ashford. Give me your phone number, and I'll call you tomorrow. I'll have Mum come in to mind the little brute, and we can really get down to it. Now I *must* go!'

'Later,' Jane murmured to me as they left. 'Lots more.'

Alan, unasked, poured us all another drink. 'Now that a man can hear himself think, can someone tell me what that was all about?'

I deferred to Lucy, who thought for a moment. 'To tell the truth, I'm not quite sure. You'll have figured out that the girl – well, woman, but I think of her as a girl – was my BFF when we were kids. She lived just down the street from me, and we did everything together. Then my family moved to Ashford and I went to a different school, and we sort of drifted apart. I missed her a lot, because she was lively and I was stodgy. I never heard a word from her after we moved to America, until my parents died and she wrote to me. Then we just sort of picked up from where we'd left off, and it was great. So Jane thought we should get together, and brought her over.' She sipped her drink. 'But I got the oddest feeling that this wasn't just a reunion, that Caroline has something on her mind. I wish she hadn't gone so soon.'

'Babies don't deal well with changes in their routine,' said the experienced father and grandfather. 'She really did need to get home to him. You can have a good long talk tomorrow and catch up on all the missing years. And speaking of catching up . . .' He fixed a meaningful stare on the kitchen door.

'Okay, okay. It'll be a scratch meal, though. This visit upset my schedule for the afternoon, and I still haven't sent those emails off to America.'

Our meal was edible, if not exciting, and when I got back to my emailing, I had a hard time concentrating. I was pretty sure Jane hadn't brought Caroline over simply to let old friends chat. Jane's actions always had purpose. I speculated. Was there some deep, dark secret in Lucy's past that Caroline could reveal? Or vice versa? That was perhaps more likely, given the characters of the two girls. But what could something so long ago have to do with a man Lucy had known only for months?

After misspelling three words in the email I was going to send to my American friends, I gave it up. Reasoning ahead of one's data was fruitless, as Sherlock Holmes once pointed out. I corrected my message, hit Send, and went to bed.

Next morning, things began to happen. The weather had changed again to picture-perfect May, but my mind wasn't any clearer, so I wrapped myself in our search once more. Both Alan and I found a bunch of emails in our inboxes, replies from America. Most of them, predictably, were of no interest, but Alan found one promising item.

'Ah,' he said, 'here's one worth exploring. The police in Bloomington received a complaint from an authority at the university. Someone was soliciting on the grounds—'

'The campus,' I interrupted.

'Yes, thank you, the campus. Which is not allowed. The

university security force responded, but the chap had gone by the time they showed up, so the matter was referred to the city police, at the insistence of the . . . dean, would it be?'

'Probably. It wouldn't normally be something the city would handle, but town–gown relationships are very important in Bloomington, since the university is by far their largest employer and source of tourism, income, whatever.'

'I see. At any rate the city did get involved and interviewed a few people this person had spoken to.'

'And who were they? Not names, I don't mean, but were they students or faculty or staff?'

'Faculty. Apparently quite important in the hierarchy, though their titles didn't mean a lot to me. They all told the same story. The chap was trying to interest them in donating to his charity in aid of COVID victims. He had an accent variously described as English or "funny", and gave his name as William Gray.'

'Bingo! "Funny" probably meaning Scottish. And if he was dealing with deans and chairmen and the like, they'd have had the kind of money he was looking for. Well, I've got one for you. One of my friends at Randolph is long retired, but she keeps up with the grapevine, and she tells much the same story. Soliciting on campus, annoyed a number of people, got out of there before any authorities could catch up with them.'

'"Them"?'

'That's the good part. There were two of them, at different times. One was William Gray. The other introduced himself as Robert Brinton.'

'Brinton? But—'

'Exactly. And listen to this! Gray delivered the same spiel as in Bloomington, but Brinton came around several days later and told a different story. According to my friend Marci, he was telling people Gray was a con man and a fraud, and if they were inclined to contribute anything, they should do it through him!'

'Betrayal! A falling-out among thieves! Good grief, woman, this begins to sound like an opera plot.'

'Maybe it wasn't betrayal, though. Maybe Campbell/Gray

wasn't pulling in enough by himself, so he sent Brinton along, all sweetness and light, to help the poor deluded donors, and incidentally get more money.'

Alan frowned. 'You think they were working together.'

I ran my hands through my hair, which made it stand up in grey spikes. 'Or not! I don't know what to think. Every new thing we learn seems to turn our ideas upside down.'

Alan sighed. 'I used to think I was good at untangling criminal schemes, but either I've lost my touch, or criminals have grown more clever. I need a break.'

Lucy, who had gone for a walk, came into the room. 'I just had a call from Carrie. She wants to meet me for lunch at the Feathers. That's on the High Street, isn't it?'

'Yes, out the west gate and just to the left. You'll like it. They have excellent pub food.'

'Would you like to come with me?'

'No, dear. You want to have a good long gabfest with your friend, and Alan and I are working on other plans. You go ahead and enjoy yourselves.'

Once she was gone, Alan turned back to me. 'The mention of pub food gave me an idea. Why don't we drive up to the university and get a bite to eat at that pub near the gate, the Bells and Motley? There's a chamber music concert in Old Hall this afternoon that should soothe our savage breasts.'

'And perhaps energize our languid brains? Excellent. Let's do it.'

I don't know if it was the pleasant atmosphere of a good pub, or the glorious concert (all baroque, my favourite period), but Alan and I came home much refreshed and ready to face our problem again. 'Let's go for a walk instead of a nap,' I proposed. 'It's such a lovely day, and I think better out in the fresh air.'

It was a perfect day. Sun, a slight breeze, lots of colour and aroma from flower beds and the blossoms of fruit trees, and lots of noise – joyful noise. The birds were of course at it in full voice, and added to that cacophony were the shouts of small children as the school day ended.

'Should we try to find some quiet place?' Alan suggested.

'I doubt there is any just now, unless we shut ourselves up

in the Cathedral, and I want to be outside. I don't really mind
the noise. I used to be in a classroom all day, remember? I
learned to ignore happy children's voices.'

So we strolled down to the river and walked along
the banks, watching the ducks and geese and avoiding the
ganders, who were inclined to belligerence in defence of
their new babies.

'I think—'

I began at the same moment that Alan said, 'It seems
to me—'

We both laughed and he deferred to me. 'I think, then, that
we're working from the wrong end, concentrating on the
crooks, Iain/William and Robert. The cops can trace their
activities much more easily than we can.'

'Great minds,' said Alan. 'I was about to say exactly the
same thing.'

'So I think we should start thinking about the victims.
After all, if the two villains have been defrauding people
for a long time, there have to be loads of folks out there
with every reason to be furious with the pair, either or both
of them.'

'Ye-es,' said Alan dubiously. 'But there's a big difference
between being furious and being murderous.'

'Of course there is. But there's fury and then there's fury.
The kind that blows up fast can dissipate fast. People take it
out in bad language and storming around, and it doesn't usually
do much harm, except to one's blood pressure. But the other
kind, the kind that worms its way into your soul and grows
there like a cancer, that kind can be truly dangerous.'

'Hmm.' By that time we'd found a handy bench to sit on,
and Alan tented his hands, pressing them to his lips in thought.
'Yes. And that sort, the malignant sort, usually begins with a
perceived injury to some beloved person or thing. A man
whose house is deliberately set on fire will rail and curse at
the arsonist, and may threaten him, but when he calms down
he'll be content with the insurance settlement and the
prison sentence that's meted out. But if his wife, or child, or
even his dog, was killed in that fire, he'll swear vengeance
and may even carry it out.'

I thought about that. 'So if we apply this to our fraud case, a victim who lost a lot of money won't feel kindly to the fraudsters, but will concentrate on getting back anything he can and seeing the crooks get punished. But . . . what would make him turn to murder?'

'The same principle, I should think. The money that was stolen was being saved to help someone he loved. Perhaps his elderly mother had to have expensive home care that her health insurance couldn't provide (since your health care system in America is so inadequate). Or his wife owed a huge debt to some crook – perhaps a gambling debt – and was under serious threat if she didn't pay. There are any number of possibilities.'

'I see. And the situation that the money could solve will just keep getting more and more critical until the poor guy snaps. Alan, that makes a lot of sense! So how are we going to look for victims? There may be hundreds of them, for all we know.'

'That's where the American authorities may be of great help. With the information we can now give them, I'm sure the . . . what did you call it, the group that regulates financial trading?'

'The SEC, Securities and Exchange Commission.'

'They may already be nosing into this bogus "charity" operation, but they can find out more with the names and dates we can give them.'

'Yes, and we can put Nigel to work, too, making Campbell's computer spit out more data. But the very best source of information about the victims would be Robert Brinton. Alan, we need to find him.'

'Yes, but I have the feeling we've already missed our best chance. Or rather, the police have.'

I sighed and nodded. 'You think he maybe killed Iain himself. At the wheel of a car with signs of collision damage.'

'Which he would have abandoned as soon as possible, and flown back to Chicago. Or somewhere. Given twenty-four hours, he could have fled to virtually anywhere on the planet. But whether he's the guilty party, or simply might know who is, he has to be found.'

TWENTY

Lucy called as we were walking home, saying she'd be having supper with Carrie and might be late getting back, so we were not to wait up for her. So it was morning before we heard about her long visit.

The day was so perfect we took our coffee into the back garden, where the animals kept us company as we sat and sipped and listened.

'It's hard to believe, but we're still not talked out,' said Lucy with a bubbling giggle. 'You'd think we were still teenagers. But gosh, we had a lot of ground to cover. Carrie had a really hard time after I moved away.'

'Her anchor was gone?'

'That, and her mum started being totally unreasonable with her, practically keeping her under lock and key.'

Alan groaned. 'Exactly *not* the way to deal with a child you think might run wild. Better to let them know you trust them, even if you have your doubts.'

'Oh, Uncle Alan, you're so right! That's the way my parents dealt with me when I got to the rebellious age. They were patient when I sassed back. They talked to me as if I were a sensible person, so most of the time I acted like a sensible person. They didn't lay down the law, but they set guidelines and let me know they were sure I would follow them. So most of the time I did, and I didn't get into much trouble. But poor Carrie!' Lucy made a 'can you believe it' gesture, flinging both arms wide and showering Watson with coffee in the process. Fortunately it wasn't very hot, and the sleepy dog only opened one eye, shook himself, and went back to sleep.

'Sorry, Aunt Dorothy!'

'No harm done. Watson's due for a bath anyway, and coffee won't hurt the grass.'

'Well, anyway, Carrie said her parents made so many rules

she felt like she was in prison. They wouldn't let her go out with her friends, even the girls she'd played with all her life. She couldn't go to the movies, couldn't go to concerts or dance parties because her parents were scared she'd start doing drugs.'

'Which meant that she did all those things on the sly and lied about it.' I shook my head.

'The thing was, she didn't really like any of it. She just wanted to have a good time with her friends. She never liked loud music or strobe lights or any of the rave scene, and pot and booze made her sick. She was just kicking against the traces, cocking a snook at her parents, showing them she'd do what she wanted. Is there more coffee, since I dumped most of mine?'

I pointed to the Thermos on the tray, and she poured some.

'Are you sure I'm not boring you?'

'Not at all,' said Alan. 'I've always enjoyed horror stories.'

Lucy made a face. 'And it's all of that. Because it was at one of these awful parties that she met the jerk. And that's when she really went off the deep end. Stopped going to school, started snorting coke, started sleeping with the jerk, even tried Ecstasy.'

'Oh, no! But that's terribly dangerous!' Alan and I had been involved some years ago in the investigation of a rave club in Cornwall and had learned about Ecstasy and its potentially lethal effects.

Lucy shuddered. 'Is it ever! But Carrie was one of the really lucky ones. She's allergic to opioids; they make her sick, as in puking all over the place. And Ecstasy, which makes most people really high, gave her horrible hallucinations. She was trying to keep taking all that junk, because El Jerko kept pressuring her. And then my parents died, and she wrote to me.'

'So you literally did save her life.'

Lucy might have picked up a lot of American attitudes and vocabulary, but she was still English enough to be embarrassed by praise. 'Oh, well, she just decided to change the way she was living.'

Because of your example, I thought but didn't say. Lucy

knew what she had done. No point in making her uncomfortable about it. 'So did she just dump the guy and the club scene and start to make a life for herself? I'd have thought that would be hard to do.'

'It was. And she couldn't do it just like that, all at once. She stopped going to the raves and taking the drugs. That was actually easy, since she hated them anyway. But it was harder to get away from the jerk.'

'Didn't he have a name?' asked Alan with some impatience.

'She never said. I think maybe she thought it would give him some . . . I don't know, dignity or something. Or maybe it's just superstition. You know, the power of a name?'

'Or maybe she just can't bear to say it, given what she thinks of him. But you said it was hard to get away from him?'

'He kept stalking her. Is that illegal here?'

'Yes,' said Alan, 'but only fairly recently. I believe the laws in the States are more comprehensive.'

'So maybe it wouldn't have been illegal then. Anyway, he wouldn't leave her alone. First tried sweet-talking her into coming back, he really needed her, nothing was any fun without her, that kind of crap. Then he started threatening her. Said he knew a guy who knew a guy who could make life tough for her.' Her face changed. She finished her coffee and put the cup down. Her hand, I noticed, wasn't entirely steady. 'The tough guy lived in Scotland, the jerk said. He wouldn't rough her up or anything crude like that. Oh, no, he was a perfect gentleman, but he had a lot of influence in high places, even in England. He had money. He could see to it that Carrie never got into the university she wanted, or got a job she wanted, or ever had a good life.'

My nerves had tightened the moment she said 'Scotland'. I raised my eyebrows.

Lucy shook her head 'She never told me a name. Maybe the jerk never told *her*. But the description sounds familiar, doesn't it?'

The animals were getting restless, and the metal framework of my lawn chair was beginning to cut into my thighs. I stood (with Lucy's help) and stretched. 'I need a bathroom after all

that coffee, and a sandwich or something. And then Watson
needs a walk. He's been giving me pitiful looks for a while now.'

We had sandwiches, and then Lucy went with me to exercise
Watson. 'You never finished Carrie's story. How did she get
away from her nasty boyfriend in the end?'

'It was actually her father. She was amazed, because he'd
been so stern and controlling for so long, and she thought
he'd never help her with anything. But he'd seen that she was
trying to straighten up, so he hired a tutor to help her finish
school, and she worked so hard she did great on her A Levels
and won a scholarship to Durham, of all exalted places. Her
parents were thrilled, I think partly because it would take her
far away from her boyfriend and her other not-so-terrific friends
here. And that really is the end of the story, the horrible part,
anyway.'

I shook my head in sympathy. 'She's had an awful time,
hasn't she? It takes a strong person to conquer the hazards
she had to face.'

'And it's my fault. If I hadn't gone away—'

'Now stop that! No, Watson, dear, I didn't mean you.' For
he had looked up, confused. 'You're a good dog. I wasn't
scolding you.' I leaned down to scratch his head. He licked
my hand, and his tail gave a wag or two. 'I was scolding you,
Lucy, but I'll have to do it in a gentler voice, or my poor dog
will get upset again. My dear child, what will it take to convince
you that you are in no way to blame for Carrie's woes?' She
started to speak, but I put up a hand. 'For a start, you had no
control over the move to America. Your parents took you, and
at that age, you had very little say in the matter. In the second
place, Carrie made her own decisions about her own behaviour. It seems her parents didn't deal with her very wisely, but
parents are human beings, just as prone to error as anyone
else. So her troubles were not their fault, either. No, the blame
falls squarely on her shoulders.'

'But she was only a kid!'

'Emotionally, yes. Most adolescents can be very childish.
You were the same age, but you were level-headed. Look,
there's never any point in assigning credit or blame. The fact
is, you and her father helped Carrie get out of the pit she'd

dug for herself, and then she took the next steps. And by the time she'd got herself back to a sensible life, it was you who lost your mind.'

'And she's come to rescue me,' Lucy murmured.

I gave her a quizzical look.

'That's why she came to talk to me, don't you get it? Jane called her because I was here for a little while, and the old dear thought we'd like seeing each other again when we had the chance. And then Carrie told her at least part of the story, about the Scotchman and all, and Jane arranged the meeting.'

'Scotsman,' I corrected automatically. 'So you think that bit was the whole point of her story?'

'Don't you? She wanted me to see that falling for a jerk can happen to anybody, even sober, serious me, and that it isn't just the girl's fault, and above all, it doesn't have to be the end of the world.'

I nodded. 'She's evening the score, you think. A rescue for a rescue.'

'Exactly.'

We'd reached the park, where I let Watson off the lead to cavort as much as his elderly little heart desired, and sat down on the bench my elderly (if artificial) knees desired. It was still early afternoon, with the older children in school, and many of the younger ones probably having their naps, so the place was relatively quiet. A good place to think.

'You know, Carrie's done more than just restore your self-respect. She's given us a possible lead to Iain's victims on this side of the Atlantic.'

Lucy was quick. 'Oh! And we want to find them, because one of them might have finally blown up.'

'Right.' I explained the conclusions Alan and I had come to. 'And it would be a lot more convenient if the possible murderer were ready to hand, so to speak.'

'Sure. But the trouble is, it was the jerk who told Carrie about the guy who knew Iain, and the jerk's in prison. And we don't even know his name.'

'We'll ask. Carrie will tell us now that we have a good reason. And then Alan will find a way to talk to him and get the name of his Scottish friend. And then we're off.'

'Chasing a wild goose, probably.'

'Perhaps. But even wild geese are sometimes useful.'

A volley of barking caught our attention. 'Oh, dear, speaking of geese!' Watson and several of the other dogs had ventured too close to a family of geese that had unwisely come ashore, and a serious attack was about to begin. The other dog owners and I rushed to rescue our canine companions, and for a while all was noise and confusion. Eventually, at the cost of a peck or two on my arms from a furious gander, I got Watson back on his lead and out of the fray.

I hadn't the heart to scold him. He'd been pecked, too, and was bleeding in a couple of places.

'Anyway, I don't think he really did anything, Aunt Dorothy, just followed the other dogs to have a look at the cute little goslings. He's sorry, aren't you, sweetie pie?'

'Yes, I'd say he's been punished enough. Come on, invalid, we'll take you home and bind your wounds.'

Fortunately Jane was home when we got there, and agreed with me that Watson didn't require the services of the vet, just some disinfectant and a couple of dressings. 'Will he try to chew them off?' asked Lucy.

'I don't think so. He's had bandages before and they never worried him. And he hates that cone thing, so I won't put one on him if I don't have to. I'll put some ointment on the problem spots so they won't itch. I hope. Poor old dog, I hope he's learned his lesson.'

'The lesson being, don't follow the crowd into danger. One that both Carrie and I had to learn the hard way.'

TWENTY-ONE

Carrie was in the middle of putting her son to bed when we phoned, but promised to call back when she had him settled, which was after we'd had a modest supper and were settled ourselves.

'This won't take long if you're worn out,' said Lucy to her

friend, putting the conversation on speaker so we could all take part.

'I'm recovering, thank you. I thought this would get easier as he got older, but now it's become a game: how long can I resist until Mum finally wins?'

'And I expect that time comes when he's too sleepy to think up more mischief,' I said, thinking about my nieces and nephews when they were small.

'So far. You can't imagine how happy I am that he's been weaned for a few months now, and I can have a restorative glass of wine.' We heard her take a swallow. 'You said you have a question for me?'

'A simple one that I hope won't bother you too much. Uncle Alan wants to talk to the jerk, find out who his buddy was, the one who knew Iain.'

'Um . . . why?'

'It would take too long to explain everything, but the idea is that the cops need to find out more about people who might have hated Iain. You can understand why.'

Carrie still wasn't sure. 'We don't know for certain it was Iain he was talking about.'

'No. But the description fits, and we'll soon find out if we're wrong. But only if Uncle Alan can talk to the jerk. Yeah, we know he's in prison. But remember Uncle Alan is a retired policeman, a big shot who still has influence. He'll be allowed to talk to the guy.'

'But will the guy talk to him? He's not the most cooperative of men. All right. His name is Jimmie Spinks. It should be spelt with a T. And I hate to tell you this, but he's in the Scrubs.'

Alan groaned and turned to me in explanation. 'Wormwood Scrubs, my dear. Possibly the nastiest facility in England. The ugly name is apt.'

'Oh, dear.'

'Oh, dear is right, Mrs Martin. I've never visited there, but I've heard horror stories. Sometimes I'm almost ready to feel sorry for the jerk.' Carrie chuckled. 'Not very often, though. But I can tell you, when I heard what it was like, after he was thrown in there, it made me even more resolved never to go back to that way of life.'

'"Scared straight", they used to call it in America,' I put in. 'Maybe still do. I'm told it can be very effective. But I must admit I'm not thrilled at the idea of Alan going there. I mean, is it dangerous?'

'I'm sorry to say that it can be, my dear. Rest assured I'll be well guarded and take every precaution.'

'But why does it have to be you? Surely one of the guards, or the warden or someone, could ask him such a simple question?' My feet were getting very cold indeed.

'Of course. But the trick is getting him to answer. At one time I was rather good with uncooperative witnesses. The carrot and the stick, you know.'

'Yes, well, back then you had a lot of authority with plenty of carrots and sticks at your disposal.'

'Quite right. And I haven't many carrots anymore, I admit. I can't offer him a reduced sentence, for example. But there are still those sticks. I can hint of more stringent living conditions, or a few more charges that might be brought against him, witnesses who were afraid to testify before, that sort of thing. How intelligent would you say he is, Mrs Carlson?'

'Oh, heavens, call me Carrie. Everyone else does. As for Stinks, he's not clever at all, though he thinks he is. And certainly not well educated. He's spent too much time behind bars, and even when he was technically in school he never studied. Ask Miss Langland.'

'I shall. That's an excellent idea. But you think he might not know a great deal about criminal law.'

'Not unless he's learned it from his fellow inmates. But he's never been good at making friends with other men. It was the girls who interested him.'

'Good. This is all very useful information, and I thank you very much indeed, Mrs— Carrie.'

'You're a doll, Carrie,' said Lucy. 'Now go back to your nice glass of wine and we'll stop bothering you.'

'See here, Lucy, how many times do I have to say you are not bothering me! I'll do anything I can to help nab whoever killed Iain. He was a jerk, too, but you thought you loved him, and you're hurting. Don't you dare accuse yourself of troubling me!'

When the call was ended I must have given a long sigh, or some other sign of distress, because Watson got up from the basket where he was sleeping with Mike and came to sit on my feet.

'Good old boy,' I said, stroking his silky ears. 'You want your people to be happy, don't you?' His tail wagged twice and he went back to sleep. 'The thing is, Alan, I'm really *not* happy about you going to that horrible place. Now that the name of the place has come up, I remember reading about riots and inspections and miserable conditions. I don't *like* it! Do you really have to go?'

He came and sat beside me on the couch and took my hand. 'No, my dear. I am under no obligation to go to Wormwood Scrubs. I have no desire to visit that despicable place, believe me, and I won't if it will cause you undue distress. I do think that I could gain some valuable information from Mr Spinks, information that we need in order to track down a murderer. If you prefer that someone else interview the man, I will suggest that to the Met.'

Lucy sat giving us worried looks.

I suddenly remembered the scene in Dorothy Sayers's *Busman's Honeymoon* when Harriet is very upset about Lord Peter's intention to investigate the murder that has taken place in the house they've just moved into. She realizes that if she insists, he will respect her wishes and drop the matter – and something in their relationship will be irrevocably damaged.

'No, Alan. No. You've let me walk into possible danger, often, when you would much have preferred to keep me safe at your side.' I managed to smile. 'Sauce for the goose, and all that. You go ahead and do as you think best. But don't you dare get hurt!'

'We do seem to be dealing with a lot with geese today,' said Lucy, which eased the tension. We all laughed, and Watson, satisfied, went back to his basket.

It was too late in the day to make arrangements for the prison visit, but I knew Alan would be on the phone to the Met first thing in the morning.

So the following morning, I got up to the sound of the cathedral bells and slipped over to Matins to pray for Alan's safety. The choir wasn't there, for some reason, so it was a spoken service, but the timeless quiet and peace of the old church and the old prayers soothed me. I left in a much happier frame of mind.

Alan, who almost always knows what I'm thinking, cocked an eyebrow when I walked into the kitchen. 'Feeling better?'

'Much, and starving. Maybe we could have a proper breakfast, just this once?'

A Proper Breakfast implies enough calories, carbs, and cholesterol to shorten our lives considerably. I nodded enthusiastically. 'But no baked beans, please,' I added, as if Alan didn't know that I've never cultivated a taste for that English breakfast oddity.

He shook his head in mock disbelief and got out the frying pan.

When Lucy came down, the kitchen was redolent of sausages, fried bread, mushrooms, and fresh coffee. The eggs were ready to cook, and the tomatoes were grilling. 'Have I died and gone to heaven?'

'Only back to England,' said Alan. 'How do you like your eggs?'

Of course the animals had to have their share. 'None of this is good for them,' I commented, cutting a small piece of sausage for Watson.

'Nor for us,' said Lucy, grinning as she slipped a crumb of scrambled egg to Mike.

'A little of what you fancy does you good,' Alan sang in his best imitation of Cockney, and I nearly choked on my coffee.

Alan went straight to his phone while Lucy and I tidied up the kitchen. 'Alan does make wonderful food,' I said as I scrubbed the frying pan, 'but I could wish he made less of a mess doing it.'

'My dad was just the same, and Mum used to have the same complaint. But maybe it's worth it. Anyway, you don't eat like this very often, do you?'

'More often when we have company. But no, in the normal run, not often. So what the heck, we can manage once in a while.'

We were putting away the last plate when Alan came to the kitchen. 'I'm off to London, ladies. I hope to be back in time for tea, but I'll call if I'm going to be later.'

'We're going with you,' I said, taking off my apron.

'No, my love. You are definitely *not* going to the Scrubs, if I have to handcuff you to the bed!'

'I didn't say anything about the Scrubs. Lucy and I are going to London for a good time!'

We went by rail, as a car in London is a terrible nuisance. There's no place to park, and the traffic is dreadful, and the congestion charge is discouraging. The train actually gets there faster anyway. We parted with Alan at Victoria Station, where he headed for the Circle Line to Embankment, where Scotland Yard now has its headquarters. Lucy and I made for the Victoria Line to change to Piccadilly, to the Knightsbridge Station and out into the bustle of London.

London is my favourite city in the world. True, it's the only big city in the world that I know well, but I know it well because I keep coming back again and again. Even when I lived in Indiana, my husband and I visited England as often as we could, and always, always spent time in London. Now that I live in Sherebury, a short railway journey away, the magnet draws me back at least once a month.

It's partly the royal pomp. Like most Anglophiles, I'm besotted with the Royal Family. I don't like them all, as people, but I love the tradition, the colour, the splendour of it all. I know that doesn't jibe well with my liberal social attitudes. Never mind. When I watch the Queen's Guards march from their barracks in Birdcage Walk over to the Palace for the Changing of the Guard, and hear the band playing, I tear up. It's one of those 'There'll Always be an England' moments.

That's not the biggest part of my infatuation with London, though. Part of it is the history, still visible in the buildings and the street names and the monuments. A lot of it is the people, the vibrant mix of native Londoners and people from virtually every country in the world who make London their home. They bring their own cuisines with them, so that you can eat any kind of food from Armenian to Zambian, including traditional British which, no matter what you've heard, can be marvellous.

Really, though, just as it's impossible to say exactly why you love a person, I can't truly explain my love of London. It simply is, and I indulge it every chance I get.

So I didn't really mind that we arrived at Harrods a few minutes before they opened. Lucy and I browsed the windows, admiring or laughing as the fashions struck us. 'How long has it been, Lucy?'

'Oh, eons. I was only eleven when we moved to America, and even when we lived in Sherebury we didn't get up very often. And almost never to Harrods. We weren't exactly rich, and I never cared about clothes a lot, or expensive ornaments or any of that. Neither did Mum. We did come up once or twice to look at the Christmas windows.'

'Well, then, be prepared for a treat. And here we go!'

The doors opened, and there we were in the magnificence of the Food Halls, perhaps the most elaborate temple in the world dedicated to the joys of the palate. Looking at all the delicacies from around the world, I became immediately hungry, despite my huge breakfast. My conscience kicked in, though, and when I led Lucy to the coffee bar, I confined myself to a cup of espresso, ignoring the pastries that called out to me.

Lucy, sympathizing with my temptations, said she wanted to explore the rest of the huge store, so we set off.

It is said you can buy anything at Harrods except a coffin, the assumption being that no patron of that exalted emporium would ever require such a thing. Certainly we saw a collection of nearly everything as we wandered, from books to jewellery to clothes to toys to furniture to wine to gifts, and everything you can imagine in between. I wanted one of those and one of those and . . . The prices, however, kept me sensible. I did buy a few Harrods souvenirs for Christmas gifts (though it wasn't even June yet), and a Union Jack teddy bear for Lucy. She got me a box of the lovely pastries I'd been trying not to drool over.

By that time I, for one, was suffering from sensory overload and sore feet, and it was well past lunchtime. 'Look, I'm hungry and tired, and it's much too expensive to eat here, even if we could get in without advance booking. Why don't we wander a bit and see if we can't find a Pret a Manger? They're all over London, and the food isn't bad.'

'Oh, we have them in Chicago now. Not exciting, but okay.'

'The next time you come to these shores I'll take you to tea at the Ritz, to make up for fast food today. I can't do it this visit; you have to book months in advance.'

We didn't have to walk far, thank goodness. We saw the familiar Pret sign only a couple of blocks down Brompton Road, on the other side of the street. There was no light, but the zebra crossing should let us cross safely, though traffic was heavy.

Lucy glanced quickly to the left and started for the centre island.

I'll hear the squeal of brakes and the screams until my dying day.

TWENTY-TWO

Lucy lay on the pavement, one foot in the roadway. She was very still and white.

A crowd gathered at once, among them a helmeted bobby. I've never been so glad to see anyone in my life. He spoke a reassuring word to me, shooed away the gawkers, and knelt to take a close look at Lucy. He touched her neck with two fingers, and then flicked her cheek. Her eyes opened.

'What—'

'You tried to get yourself killed, is what,' said the policeman. 'A miracle you didn't manage it.'

She raised her head and tried to sit up.

He gently pushed her head back down. 'No, love. Not till we know how much damage is done.'

'But what *happened*? The crossing was clear. I looked.'

That was enough to proclaim her nationality. 'Ah. You're a

Yank. You looked the wrong direction.' He sighed. 'Happens all the time.'

'She did,' I said with a gulp. 'I tried to catch her, but the car was very close. He tried to stop, but . . .' I couldn't say any more.

'All right, we can sort it out later. Just now the question is, ambulance or not?'

'I'm fine,' said Lucy combatively. 'I've torn my slacks, and skinned my knee and maybe my elbow, but I'm okay. Everything works.' She wiggled her fingers and feet. 'My head landed on my purse, so it's okay. My head, I mean. The purse is probably done for. And . . . oh! My Harrods bag!'

One of the passers-by, who had picked it up from the street, now looked in it. 'Nothing breakable, was there, love?'

'No, it was all soft stuff. But Dorothy! Your pastries!'

'Good grief, child, don't worry about them. I'm just grateful you're not badly hurt.'

'Still,' said the bobby, 'we need to be sure.'

A bystander stepped forward. 'Constable, I'm a doctor. If you'll allow me to do a brief examination . . .'

The constable was glad to step aside, and everyone watched while the gentleman prodded bones and looked at Lucy's eyes and asked her a few questions.

'She'll do,' he said. 'Best get her cleaned up and in bed as soon as possible. She's going to be very sore for a while. Is your hotel nearby?'

'We're from Sherebury. At least I am, and Lucy is visiting me. It's kind of a long walk to Victoria Station; do you suppose someone could get us a taxi? We could get some Band-Aids there – I mean plasters – and so on.'

A couple of other policemen had arrived on the scene; one was in a cruiser and said he would take us. It took three people to get poor Lucy on her feet and keep her there; she was pretty shaky.

'All right, miss, it's just this way—'

'Miss Bowman!' The loud cry came from the doorway of the house behind us. The speaker was a tall, impressive-looking man who made his way through the small crowd, which parted for him like the Red Sea. 'Miss Bowman, what happened?'

With some difficulty, Lucy focussed on his face. 'Mr Frankson?'

We didn't go to the railway station with the policeman. Mr Frankson, whose name I finally remembered as one of Lucy's donors, insisted on whisking us in a taxi to Claridge's. I had been there only once before, on a rather fraught mission that kept me from seeing much of its grandeur. Now Lucy and I were the guests of a guest and as such were treated like royalty. (Or like the way I assume royalty might be treated.) It was a pity that I was too concerned about Lucy to pay much attention.

Claridge's is not the sort of establishment that expects to find a guest to be accompanied by a dishevelled, dirty, and indeed bleeding, young woman. The doorman, or whatever His Magnificence was called, showed nothing but impeccable courtesy. 'Good afternoon, Mr Frankson. Do you require some assistance with the young lady?'

'Thanks, George, but we can manage. Sorry about . . .' He gestured to the blood that was still dripping, slowly, on the immaculate carpet of the lobby.

'It is of no matter, sir. I will send our physician up to your room.'

Mr Frankson nodded his thanks, and we stepped into the waiting elevator.

The doctor was waiting for us when we got there. Also a maid with extra sheets and towels. In short order Lucy was undressed, bathed, anointed and bandaged, put into a lush terrycloth bathrobe, and settled in the huge bed with a glass of wine from the well-stocked bar in the room, the doctor having discouraged other painkillers. 'They can encourage the bleeding. The wine will settle her nerves and lessen the pain. Only one glass, though.' They withdrew, and I took a deep breath for the first time in what felt like hours.

'Are you really okay?' I ventured.

'Really. I feel silly about all the fuss. Aside from scrapes and bruises, I'm fine. Truly. Only I'm really hungry, and I expect you are, too.'

'Oh, dear. Maybe that's part of the reason I'm so shaky. I thought it was just a nervous reaction.'

'That's a problem we can easily deal with. Lunch or tea, or both?' Mr Frankson picked up the phone and ordered what sounded like enough food for a regiment.

'Now,' he said as he hung up, 'I want to know what the hell is going on. For a start, what are you doing in London, Miss Bowman?'

'Lucy, please. Business etiquette feels pretty silly when I'm lying in your bed!'

He grinned. It made him look much less formidable, though the surroundings still intimidated. I had no idea what the tab would be for a suite at Claridge's, but it was quite apparent that this was a man of wealth, power, and influence.

'Then I'm Fred. And I'm waiting for an answer.'

'The short answer, if you'll allow me to intervene, is that nothing much happened today. I brought Lucy to London – I'm her friend and honorary aunt, Dorothy Martin—'

'And guardian angel,' Lucy interrupted.

'Brought her to London to shop and get to know this marvellous city a little bit. We had just left Harrods and were crossing the street when Lucy looked the wrong way at a crosswalk and got hit by a car. No one's fault except mine. I forgot to remind her about English traffic patterns.'

'You're quite sure it was accidental?'

'Quite sure,' said Lucy. 'Why would you think it wasn't?'

'Miss Bowman – Lucy – some very odd things have been happening. First, your friend with the two names, Iain Campbell-slash-William Gray, is killed in a hit-and-run in London. Carrying, incidentally, a passport in the assumed name. At least, I suppose Gray was the assumed name?'

'It took us a little while to figure that out, but yes.'

Our food arrived just then, and I'm not sure Lucy's relieved sigh was entirely a reaction to the thought of sustenance. She wasn't finding this conversation easy.

Frankson let her eat in peace for a few minutes and then began with his list again. 'I hadn't heard about his death until you called me, nor had I really thought about the man who looked so very much like him. But then I began remembering this and that, small things, but they began to make a pattern, one that I didn't care for. You go to England. It was easy to learn why. Parkwood is very proud of you, by the way. Not many of their people get invited to lecture at an English university. Then the binomial wonder goes to England a couple of days later and gets killed in what is probably not an accident, and suddenly the American media go silent about the matter. I begin to wonder why.

'I also begin to get phone calls. First from friends, fellow businessmen who were getting worrisome little signals that some of their recent investments might not be quite secure. Some of the signals seemed to have their roots in Scotland. Some in England. Some, funnily enough, in Indiana, not known as a red-hot centre of the financial world.

'The phone call that tipped the balance was from a very good friend, who happens to be employed by the SEC. He was able to be much more specific than the others. He said quite flatly that there was going to be an investigation into the dealings of one Iain Campbell and one William Gray, who were thought to have engaged in insider trading, for a start, and downright fraud. He was very grateful when I could tell him that they were investigating only one man operating under two names. And in return he told me what I think he would not have revealed otherwise. He said there was a related investigation, just beginning, into someone named Robert Brinton.'

Lucy was sipping her wine. She choked and nodded at me.

While she was recovering, I told Frankson. 'Robert Brinton, we just discovered, married Iain Campbell a few weeks ago.'

Fred Frankson was good at handling shock. His eyes turned steely, but his voice was calm when he said, 'I thought Campbell was engaged to Lucy.'

'So did she.'

Lucy had stopped coughing. Her voice was hoarse, but she managed to say, 'He was married, or just about to marry, when he asked me to marry him. Last I heard, bigamy is illegal, too. *And* a fraud.'

'He was a busy boy, wasn't he?' Frankson's voice was very dry. 'Mrs Martin, I understand you and your husband have been investigating the whole mess.'

'Entirely unofficially, along with several other people. If you know that much, you know that my husband was once a senior police official, and though he's long retired, he still knows a lot of people.'

The man looked at me with what wasn't quite a grin. 'And you are a retired teacher, I believe. Have you and your team come to any conclusions?'

'Only guesses, some probable, others far-fetched.'

'All right, I'll hazard a guess of my own. Are you putting your money on Robert Brinton?'

'We were staking almost all of it on him. At short odds.'

'Aunt Dorothy, I would never have suspected you of betting on the horses!'

'I don't. Neither does Alan. I'm not even sure I've got the jargon right. Isn't the favourite always given short odds? And does that mean you don't get much if he wins?'

'Correct on all counts,' said Frankson. 'May I ask why you were offering short odds on Brinton?'

Lucy took a swallow of water and looked him straight in the eye. 'You may, if we, Aunt Dorothy and I, may ask why it's any concern of yours?'

I frowned. 'My dear, that isn't very polite.'

'No, it isn't,' Frankson agreed. 'But it's a legitimate question, though it might have been better phrased, and it has a reasonable answer. Two answers. First, I am very much an interested party, in the financial sense, as my good friends stand to lose a bundle to the chicanery of those two men. Second, I have taken a personal interest in the matter. I very much dislike the idea of a decent, intelligent young woman being used as a patsy for a couple of crooks. I especially dislike their utter disregard for her safety and happiness. Can you wonder that I was disturbed to find you the victim of yet another traffic accident?' He rose to pour himself a whisky, and my phone rang.

'Alan,' I said, looking at the display, and answered. 'What's up, dear?'

'Dorothy, are you all right? They tell me there was an accident—'

'I'm fine,' I interrupted. 'So is Lucy. There was a minor

accident, but a friend of Lucy's took us to his suite at Claridge's, and we're relaxing in the lap of luxury. Who told you about the accident?'

'The Met. Of course it was reported, and seeing the names, a friend passed it along to me.'

'Well, they exaggerated grossly, so calm down. What are you doing at the Yard?'

Both pairs of eavesdropping ears perked up sharply.

'Just passing along some information. Who is there with you?'

'Lucy and Mr Frankson, our rescuer.'

'I'll tell you more later. I won't be home for a couple of hours, probably. See you then.'

Lucy opened her mouth. I shook my head. 'He didn't tell me much, just that he was pursuing the investigation. How are you feeling, Lucy?'

She took the hint. 'Just achy. Not bad, actually. This helped.' She held up her wine glass.

'Well, I'm sorry you didn't end up seeing much of London, but I think it's time we got you home. Mr Frankson, you've been so kind, but we're both ready for a nap. Could you do us one more kindness and get us a cab to the station?'

I thought he might protest, but he agreed at once. 'I fear your clothes are in bad shape, Lucy. Suppose you put on underwear, for the sake of decency, and perhaps your blouse, and wear the bathrobe as a coat. The slacks are really not fit to wear.'

'I'll look peculiar, but I don't suppose British Rail, or whatever it is now, will mind. Thank you, Fred.'

'I'll be in touch.'

He took us down in the elevator, packed our bundles in, and gave instructions to the driver. I didn't pay much attention to the passing scene until I noticed that the familiar buildings, and the familiar traffic, had given way to houses and apartment buildings and rather depressing suburbia. I knocked on the window separating us from the driver. 'Um . . . where are we going?' I couldn't keep a tremor out of my voice.

'The gent told me to take you to Sherebury, luv, said as you'd give me the address when we got there. Couldn't see the young lady being happy on the train.'

I sat back. 'Good grief, Lucy. A cab all the way home! What must it be like to be rich!'

'He's been really nice to us, hasn't he? And I don't even know him that well. We only met in person a couple of times before COVID made everything virtual. He was always polite, though, and always generous. I guess he can afford it.'

'Looks that way, doesn't it?'

We covered another mile or two before Lucy spoke again. 'Aunt Dorothy, what did Uncle Alan really tell you? I could see you didn't want me to ask in front of Mr . . . of Fred.'

'It was more what he didn't say. He was calling from the Yard, as you gathered. Apparently he'd seen the jerk and got some useful information. That's really all. I'm sure he'll tell us more when he gets home, which may not be for a while. Lucy, do you trust Mr Frankson?'

She thought about it. 'I'm not sure. He's kind, and he's generous, but so was Iain, I thought. He's smooth. So was Iain.'

'Ye-es. But he isn't what I'd call charming. There are a few too many rough edges for that. I've probably told you I never trust obvious charm.' I sighed. 'I'm not sure about him, either, though I'm leaning in his favour. Lucy, I hope you're not going to let one awful experience put you off men for life.'

'I'm not . . . Aunt Dorothy! You're not suggesting that Fred Frankson is interested in me, in that way, I mean! Because I'm sure not interested in him.'

'No, of course not. Don't be silly.'

As Alan said, I can lie beautifully in a good cause.

TWENTY-THREE

Home. We bestirred ourselves to feed the animals, who had greeted us according to their various natures. Sam and Emmy snubbed us, furious that we had deserted them all day, Watson was overjoyed that we were back, and Mike just wanted his dinner. Once that chore was done, I made tea for both of us, since Lucy was forbidden any more alcohol for a while, and certainly neither of us needed anything to eat. Then we collapsed in the parlour and were very nearly asleep when Alan walked in.

'I see we've all had a stimulating day,' was his comment as he crossed the room, patted Watson's head, and poured himself a whisky.

'You have no idea,' I retorted. 'So stimulating that we're nearly done in.' I yawned widely. 'Do you want to hear about it or have something to eat? I warn you, it's slim pickings.'

'I had a sandwich on the train.'

'Yummy, I'll bet.'

'Edible. I wasn't hungry, after . . . a rather trying day.'

That wasn't what he'd started to say. I couldn't tell whether he wanted to talk about it or not, so I nudged Lucy. 'Do you want to tell him about our day, or shall I?'

'You,' she said, stroking Mike's ears as he purred in her lap.

'Okay, *Reader's Digest* version. Went to Harrods. Window-shopped.'

'Which was just about all we could afford in that place,' Lucy commented.

'Bought a couple of souvenirs after touring the store. Can you believe Lucy'd never been there before? It was well after lunchtime when we ran out of steam, so we headed down the street to a Pret. It was on the other side of the street, so Lucy started to cross at a zebra crossing, only she looked the wrong way and got hit by a car coming from the right.'

'Not hit, really,' she protested, 'just nudged and knocked down. It was an *accident*, Uncle Alan, and my own stupid fault, as I kept trying to tell Fred.'

So then we had to explain about Fred. Alan, whose memory is a lock-box, knew immediately who he was. 'The American millionaire who told you about William Gray.'

'After what we saw today, I'd say "millionaire" is a gross understatement.' I rolled my eyes. 'I told you he stopped to see if Lucy was all right, and then took us to his hotel to pamper her. Alan, he's staying in a suite at Claridge's. He sent us home in a taxi. I mean, from Claridge's to our front door! *And* he's on friendly terms with someone from the SEC. To be vulgar, he's rolling in it.'

'But he's *nice*,' said Lucy. 'He doesn't throw his wealth around, to show off. Actually, he does a lot of good with it. Trust me, I really do know about his philanthropy. It's genuine, not like Iain's.'

'You seem to have made up your mind about him,' I said.

'Am I missing something here?' asked Alan.

Lucy and I spoke at the same time. She gestured to me. 'We thought, both of us, that he might be taking more interest in the whole mess than seemed reasonable, and couldn't decide if we quite trusted him. I even began to wonder—'

'Aunt Dorothy thinks he fancies me. I'm sure that's not it. I think he's just being sort of fatherly, trying to protect me from the big bad world, especially the big bad con men.'

'Fatherly,' said Alan blandly. 'How old did you say he is?'

'I didn't. I never thought about it.' She looked down at the kitten.

'Dorothy?'

'Mid-thirties, I'd say. He might seem a little older because he's so well-dressed and self-confident. No, that's not the right word. Poised, perhaps. He seems comfortable in his own skin.'

'Ah. Well, at any rate he's looking out for my girl, and I'm prepared to like him for that alone, if nothing else.' He sat back and sipped his whisky. 'Did he tell you why he's in London?'

'Nosing into the Campbell accident. He thinks it's pretty fishy, and he's uneasy about Lucy's involvement. But you haven't told us a thing about your day. I gather it was productive?'

He tossed off the rest of the whisky and sat silent for a while. When he spoke, his voice had aged. 'I'm not going to tell you about my visit to the prison. Trust me, you don't want to know. I wish I thought I could forget the details.' He reached for his glass and found it empty. I refilled it.

'I will say only that I pray I never come closer to Hell than I did today. But you want me to tell you about my conversation with Spinks.' A sip from his glass. 'Lucy, you tell your friend from me that she should thank God on her knees every day that she was able to break away from him. I've known a lot of villains in my time, but he's the vicious sort that, in the old days, would have ended up on the gallows.'

'But what has he actually done?' I asked. 'I mean, what crime did he commit that sent him to that awful place?'

'What hasn't he done? Jane told us he began his career with petty theft and quickly got into dealing drugs. Car theft, robbery with violence, rape. And intimidation. You can tell Carrie, Lucy, that there never was any Scottish nemesis. Spinks made him up to try to keep her in line.' Alan reached out a hand to Lucy and then went on.

'He was very clever, and had enough money to hire a good lawyer, who got him off several times. This time there was no hope. An eyewitness saw him rape and murder an old woman in Hyde Park.'

'No! That's . . . How did the witness get away with her life?'

'His life. It was a man, a big burly one. He has a job that doesn't get him home until after midnight, and he was taking his dog for a walk just before they both went to bed when he heard screams. The dog is very well trained. And very large. He didn't bark, but he led his master to the bridge over the Serpentine, where . . .' Another sip of whisky. 'Spinks was just about ready to shove the woman's body into the water when the dog attacked, not to do any real damage, but to make sure Spinks was going nowhere. The witness called 999, and the police came in force.'

Alan set the glass down, still half full. Apparently even good whisky couldn't take the taste out of his mouth.

Lucy had turned pale, as pale as I've ever seen a face. 'And this is the man Carrie . . .' She couldn't finish.

'She is truly fortunate to have escaped him.'

'He's a monster!'

She was shaking. I'm not one to ignore medical advice, but there are times when exceptions are advisable. I made another pot of tea with all possible speed and poured Lucy a cup liberally laced with brandy and sugar. The interval gave her a little time to compose herself, and when we were all settled again, Alan spoke with deliberation.

'I seldom issue orders, but I'm doing so now. Neither you, nor Lucy, nor Carrie is to take any part in any dealings with this man. Understood?'

We meekly acquiesced. I was just making a mental reservation along the lines of 'unless absolutely necessary' when I saw the look in Alan's eyes and the set of his mouth. He seemed to be staring into my very soul. I abandoned the reservation. There can be such a thing as too much understanding between spouses.

No one had an appetite. All were exhausted. We went up to bed before the evening light had quite faded from the sky.

None of us wanted to get up in the morning. Memories of the day before hung heavily over us, and so did the weather. The air was still warm, but humid and oppressive, with a storm threatening.

'Something's going to happen,' said Lucy over coffee. 'I can feel it, and so can the animals.'

The cats were certainly jittery, even little Mike with his brief experience of the world. Watson was let out and came back in as soon as possible, whining a complaint about, I assumed, life in general. 'I'm with you, old boy. This is a day to forget, even before it starts.'

Alan said nothing, just brooded over *The Times*.

Lucy and I were clearing up the breakfast dishes when her phone warbled. She glanced at the caller ID. 'Oh my gosh, it's Mr Frankson. I don't know whether to answer, or not.'

'Answer,' I said. 'You never know.'

She caught it at the last minute. 'Mr Frankson. What a surprise!'

'It's Fred, remember? I called to see how you're doing. And before you say you're just fine, it's a real question. Have you discovered any injuries you were hiding before?'

Lucy had to laugh at that. 'Nothing, truly. Except for scrapes and some spectacular bruises, I'm perfectly okay. Aside from the damage to my ego, that is.'

'Good. That will heal, along with the other wounds. Now, I also called you with some information you may find useful. Is Mrs Martin with you?'

'Yes, and Uncle Alan, too.'

'Excellent. If you could turn on your speaker, we can save some time.'

Lucy made a face at both of us, but put the phone on speaker.

'Now, Lucy, you and Mrs Martin know that I came to London to see what I could find out about Campbell, in either of his incarnations. When you told me about his marriage to Brinton, the witch's brew clouded up considerably. I take it theirs was a bona fide marriage?'

'Yes. One of our people looked up the certificate. They were legally married in Chicago.' I got up to get more coffee.

'And I'm sure you all speculated about why they took that step.'

'There are a number of possible reasons,' said Alan in his driest voice. 'None of them very creditable.'

'No. And I happened, this morning, to learn something else discreditable. My friend from the SEC called me.'

'On a Saturday?'

'Indeed. A Saturday afternoon there, to boot. He's really been digging into the Brinton case, and when I told him about the marriage, his reaction was . . . interesting, shall we say.'

'I imagine he thought of all sorts of ramifications in terms of testimony and so forth,' I speculated.

'Principally "and so forth". Because, you see, Robert Brinton has been married for seven years – to a woman – and has two children.'

'Oh, wow!' Lucy shouted loudly enough that Mike was disturbed and jumped down in annoyance. 'Oh, *wow*! I mean, that's just the last straw! You think things can't get any more weird, and then . . . oh, wow!'

'Well-educated, intelligent, articulate,' I murmured, but Frankson heard me.

'I have to admit that my response was equally inarticulate, and profane as well. But the point is—'

'The point,' said Alan, 'is that Campbell's marriage was never valid, because it was bigamous. And Brinton knew that. So whatever devious motive prompted the charade, it has to be attributed to Campbell. He thought he could profit; he could not, financially or otherwise. And Brinton knew it, and knew he couldn't benefit, either.'

'So why did Brinton agree to it?' I was holding my head in utter confusion.

'That's the question, isn't it?'

'One of them,' said Frankson. 'The other is: where *is* Brinton?'

TWENTY-FOUR

Where is Brinton? That question haunted all of us for the next several days. The Metropolitan Police were looking for him. The Federal Bureau of Investigation were looking for him, in cooperation with the Securities and Exchange Commission. Police in Chicago and various Indiana cities were looking for him. Passport authorities in both countries were combing their records. It seemed impossible that he could have vanished so completely, but no trace of him could be found.

Alan wasn't at all happy with the situation. 'He came to England two days before Campbell's death. We know that. His passport was scanned at departure from O'Hare and arrival at Heathrow. After that, nothing. He hasn't stayed at any London hotel that the Met can find. It isn't possible to check every pub and hotel and B & B in the country, but a national enquiry has gone out.'

'And I suppose he's been seen in every county in England, and on into Scotland and Wales.'

'Of course, and every single report has to be checked. They can't keep this up forever; there simply isn't enough manpower. And of course he hasn't been charged with anything, only "wanted for questioning", so the smaller forces are losing interest.'

'We're sure he hasn't left the country?'

'As sure as we can be. He hasn't left from any of the major

air or sea ports. Assuming he has no problem with money, he could have bribed a private pilot to fly him somewhere with no formalities like passports.'

'If he's been doing dodgy stock trading for years, not to mention the charity scam, it's more than likely that he has money. And Alan, if he did that, isn't it a sure admission of guilt?'

'Not legally, but fleeing as a sign of guilt is very persuasive to a jury. If we could ever find him and charge him and get him in front of a jury!'

We were sitting around the kitchen table drinking more coffee than was good for us and racking our brains. It had been a week since Lucy's accident in London, and her scrapes were almost healed. Ah, youth. The last time I skinned a knee, the signs were still visible for months.

'If he's staying with a friend, he could be almost anywhere in the UK and never be found until he wants to be.' Lucy had said more or less the same thing several times before. So had we all.

'It would help if we had any idea who Brinton's English friends might be. Or even why he came to England in the first place. I suppose somebody's talked to his wife.'

'Yes. Several agencies have been in touch with her. No luck. If she knows where he is, she's not saying. He only told her he was going to England on business. She doesn't know what business. No, he didn't say when he'd be back. No, he hasn't called or emailed, but he seldom does when he's away.' Alan picked up his empty cup, put it down again with a look of loathing, and shook his head when I gestured at the pot. 'I may never sleep again as it is.'

'I wish I could have heard one of those interviews with Mrs Brinton. Your quick summary makes it sound as if she's not at all concerned that her husband is missing and being sought by the police. I'd be frantic!'

'How old are the kids?' asked Lucy. 'Because I think a lot depends on that. If they're really little, she's maybe so busy being a mum that she doesn't have time to think about much else.'

'Or just the opposite.' I put my own coffee aside. 'I would

think she'd be worried sick about their welfare if they're really young. What if something's happened to him? What if he never comes home and she has to raise these babies all by herself? That kind of thing. If they're older, school age, say, the prospect wouldn't be quite so awful. Maybe. Where does she live, anyway?'

'The Chicago area. North, I think the report said.'

'Evanston?'

'No, that wasn't it. If it matters, I've written it down somewhere.'

'Not Winnetka?'

'Yes, that was it.'

Lucy and I groaned in unison. Alan frowned a question while he took his notebook out of his pocket.

'The thing is, dear heart, that Winnetka is one of the most expensive places to live in the area. In the state, for that matter. The family definitely has money, which means . . . what does it mean?'

'Could mean anything. Almost certainly, it means that Mrs Brinton needn't face immediate worries about the children's welfare, even if her husband never comes home. However.' Alan tented his fingers in lecturing mode. 'It appears the SEC have serious doubts about how that wealth was obtained. If fraud can be proved, criminal sentences and/or civil lawsuits could wipe out most of it.'

'In other words, Mrs B could find herself out on her ear, and her Sheridan Road mansion only a cherished memory.' Lucy didn't sound very sorry. 'The kids might have to go to public schools. Oh, the shame of it!'

'How do you know she lives on Sheridan Road?' Alan had found the information he sought, and his voice was suddenly sharp.

'Oh, Uncle Alan, I'm not trying to pull some kind of fast one! The thing is, all the gazillionaires live on Sheridan Road! It's right on the lake. Lake Michigan?' She looked at Alan doubtfully, and he nodded his assurance that he did, indeed, know about Lake Michigan and its significance to Chicago.

'Well, so you'll know it's absolutely the most desirable address you could have. And I'm not kidding about mansions.

Some of them look like castles, honestly. Of course there are really nice houses on other streets, too, priced in the millions, but the genuine Gotrocks families live on Sheridan.'

'So now we have a good idea of the size of Brinton's bank account. And what does that tell us?'

Sometimes Alan sounds just like a schoolteacher: the leading question intended to make students think.

'Let's suppose,' I said slowly, 'that our speculations about Brinton's financial speculations – or peculations, if you prefer—'

That was greeted by groans.

'It's the appropriate word, I insist. Anyway, if we're right, Robert Brinton's gazillions, to use Lucy's estimation, might soon vanish into the hands of the law. And he and his family would then, to quote Lucy again, be out on their ears. I can't imagine that Mrs Brinton would be too happy about that. And yet she seemed unconcerned when questioned about his absence. Maybe she detests the man and is delighted that he may be vanishing from her life. But what about his money? Will she be equally delighted to see that go?'

'Maybe she has money of her own,' suggested Lucy. 'What do we know about her?'

'Very little,' said Alan, 'depending upon whom you mean by "we". The various authorities involved have passed along nothing to me about her, personally.'

'Well, then.' Lucy picked up her phone.

'Calling your Chicago friends?' I queried.

'Good grief, no! They'd kill me. It isn't even six yet by their time. No, I think Nigel is our man.'

She reached his voicemail, and left an urgent message.

'Don't forget he's busy with that big project for the university. They're the ones that pay him, after all.'

'Oh, I know, and I shouldn't expect him to be at our beck and call all the time, but I'm just so *frustrated*! There are so many threads dangling, and there doesn't seem to be anything we can do about any of them!' Watson trotted over to ease his friend's worries, sitting on her feet, and of course Mike followed.

'There's a tool we often use, Dorothy and I,' said Alan

calmly, 'when we're stuck. We haven't tried it yet, have we, love?'

I looked at him with a questioning frown and then slapped my forehead. Watson looked up to see if he needed to comfort me, instead, but decided I was okay when I spoke. 'Of course! How stupid of me. A list! Where's my purse?'

Alan got it for me from the windowsill (and what it was doing there I couldn't imagine), and I pawed through it until I found my notebook.

'Um . . .' ventured Lucy. 'I don't get it. A shopping list?'

'More like lost and found, really. We make lists of everything we can think of that's pertinent to whatever we're working on, and see if we can find some patterns. It doesn't always work, but often it helps us. This is probably going to be a long one, because, as you say, there are a lot of threads. Now, where shall we start?'

'With Iain,' said Lucy as Alan suggested 'With Campbell.'

'That makes sense. We usually start with the victim, sometimes with the chief suspect. As Iain is both victim and one of the villains in this piece, he's definitely the centre of it all.' I made a heading at the top of the page. 'What do we know about him? Really know, I mean, not suspect.'

'Start with background. Born in Scotland of wealthy parents, roughly thirty-two years ago. Educated – do we know anything about his education?'

'Only that he did not attend Northwestern, as he claimed.' Lucy tried to keep the bitterness out of her voice.

'Right. But we also know that he learned impressive computer skills somewhere, so we can posit a technical school, either on this side of the Atlantic, or the other.'

'Alan, do we know when he came to America? Not when he said he did, but really?'

'I have it here somewhere.' He leafed through his own notebook. 'Well, this doesn't say when he came, but he was granted American citizenship in . . . oh, only two years ago.'

'And that process can take quite a while,' said Lucy. 'I should know! My parents got their green cards almost right away, because Dad's job in research was considered essential.

But even after that, they had to live in the country five years before they could apply for citizenship. They had just got their new passports when they died.'

'And were you young enough to be grouped in with them? I don't know how these things work in the States.'

'Yes, it's all pretty complicated, but I qualified.'

'So Iain may have been quite young when he went to the States, in his late teens. And we don't know what he did, what his occupation was, I mean.' Alan frowned.

'Or even how he got in. Unless someone's coming to fill a job, or get married, or is sponsored by somebody, it isn't always easy. Or there's always education. But Uncle Alan, why do we care? None of this will help us figure out who killed him.'

'Background, my dear. There might be contacts there, people who would know people. A policeman never knows what information might prove useful. I imagine the Social Security people could help us with some of this, and as it happens I have a friend who works for the SSA, or used to. He may be retired now, but I think I still have his mobile number. He lives in Washington, DC. Is it late enough there now, Lucy, that I could call without getting him out of bed?'

'Depends on whether he likes to sleep late. I'd say wait a while, if you want him in a good mood.'

'I agree.' I stood, irritating Emmy, who was sleeping next to me. 'I'm hungry. Whatever time it is in Washington, it's lunchtime here. I'll go see what I can find to make a meal.'

'Oh, Aunt Dorothy, don't bother. How about I spring for pizza? Only no sweetcorn or pineapple! Does anybody around here make a real American pizza?'

'As in Naples, Indiana? Or maybe Rome, Illinois?' I tried to look innocent.

'No, more like Chicago, Italy. Anyway, dear Auntie, did you know pizza originated in China?'

'You're making it up.'

'Not. The *New York Times* says so. Anyway, where's the best place in Sherebury? And do they deliver?'

After some discussion, Lucy drove to a place we liked – no, they did not deliver – and we sat down to a delectable, artery-clogging meal.

'Well, it wasn't quite Uno's, but it wasn't bad. Uncle Alan, when you come to Chicago I'll take you out for the best pizza in the world!'

'Two inches thick, at least,' I said. 'Enough calories and cholesterol to strike us dead on the spot. I love it.'

'Yes, well, speaking of being stricken dead,' said Alan, groaning as he stood up, 'we have a bit of unfinished business here. I'm going to call Washington while somebody tries Nigel again.'

Nigel promised to find out everything possible about Robert Brinton's wife, as soon as he had a spare moment. Alan's contact said he would search Social Security records, but warned it might take a while. 'There are levels on top of levels of security, not to mention that government computers are always the oldest and slowest in the world. But I'll get what you want. Eventually.' The Washington man sighed and rang off.

I turned to a new page in my notebook. 'Let's abandon Iain for the moment and work on somebody else. I vote for Brinton.'

Alan shook his head. 'I vote for returning to a thread we seem to have dropped: the victims of Campbell and Brinton. Their names must be legion.'

'But we don't know any names,' I objected.

'We have contacts, though,' said Lucy. 'Are you forgetting Fred? Mr Frankson?'

'Oh, I had, actually. Well, we can get in touch with him later. Meanwhile there are categories. Let's see: people he defrauded with his bogus charity. How do we track them down?'

'It won't be easy,' Lucy said with a sigh. 'For one thing, a good many of them won't complain.'

'But if they know their money was stolen . . .' I objected.

'But if they know that, Aunt Dorothy, they will also know that they made fools of themselves by trusting a con man. And people hate to admit that, even to themselves. Especially men.' She grinned at Alan. 'Especially men with money.'

Alan grinned back. 'Then I don't need to worry. But I'm seeing a problem with this approach. If the victims are more concerned about their image than their money, perhaps the money isn't all that important to them. In that case, they might not fit into the category Dorothy and I have been considering, people who had badly needed the money that was stolen. Would a wealthy victim be angry enough to run a man down?'

'Oh.' Lucy and I looked at each other.

'Do you have any idea, Lucy, what level of "contributions" he was soliciting?'

She thought about it, absently stroking Mike's soft little head. 'He said something once, when we were talking about our different approaches to fundraising. Even a small college needs incredible amounts of money to keep going, so I was – I am – going after the big bucks. Of course we're very nice to an alum who sends us fifty bucks, the widow's mite and all that, but the donations I personally go for are the fifty thousands and up. And Iain said he wished his donors were in that class, but charity giving was more on the widow's mite end.'

'That's not proof of anything, of course,' said Alan the policeman, 'but it's an indication.'

'Unless, of course, Iain was lying. As he had been known to do. Even if he was telling the truth at the time – when was this, Lucy?'

'Oh, gosh, only a little while after we met. Last November, maybe?'

'So things might have changed since then. He could have been testing the waters with small requests and then upped the ante.'

'Your English, my dear, is deteriorating hourly. It must be the Yank influence.'

I tossed a cushion at him. Of course that started Watson off on a chase. Mike, who hadn't yet learned that a cat is too dignified for such games, joined in and jumped on Sam, who responded with loud feline profanity, which woke Emmy, who . . .

When order was finally restored, I was sore from laughter which had turned into hiccups. The parlour was a wild jumble of newspapers, magazines, pizza boxes, and other assorted debris. Someone's phone rang.

'Oh, gosh, I think that's mine, but where is it?' Lucy pawed through a heap of cushions while Alan and I searched piles of assorted paper. He finally found it in a corner and tossed it to Lucy, just as it stopped ringing.

'Chicago,' she said, looking at the displayed number. 'Don't know who, and there's no voicemail, but I guess I'd better find out. Might be a donor; you never know.' She punched this and that and got reconnected.

'Hello, this is Lucy Bowman.'

'Lucy, Fred Frankson. I was afraid I had the wrong number.'

'No, I just couldn't find my phone. Long story. What can I do for you?'

'It's more what I might be able to do for you. I may have a few leads to your murderer.'

'Oh, wow!' She looked up at us. 'Fred. He has some ideas. Shall I—'

I nodded emphatically; Lucy turned back to the phone.

'Look, Fred, Dorothy and Alan would love to have you come over and talk about it. Are you in London?'

'No, I took a chance you'd be available and drove to Sherebury. Can you recommend a good hotel?'

'You couldn't do better than the Rose and Crown. It's a very old inn in the Cathedral Close, not exactly in the Claridge's class, but very pleasant. Go to the Cathedral; anybody will show you. And Dorothy and Alan live only a few yards away. Phone me when you get there.'

'And we can ply him with liquor and great food and pick his brains!' she enthused as she rang off.

'Correction,' said Alan. 'He can ply us. No sense letting that fortune go to waste.'

TWENTY-FIVE

I t was a pity we'd gorged on pizza, because the Rose and Crown does an excellent lunch, but we settled for soft drinks while Frankson quaffed his ale and devoured his Scotch egg.

'I've been talking to some of my friends,' he said between bites of his appetizer. 'Not very happy campers, any of them. They're furious that they were taken in, more so because they stand to lose important money.'

'Would they tell you all this, do you think, if they had carried their anger to a criminal degree?' Alan spoke softly, looking around to make sure no one was nearby. Peter had put us in a remote corner of the bar, and it was well past lunchtime. Even Max, the cushiony British Blue who fathered most of the kittens in town, was asleep in a comfy old leather chair. No one was paying us any attention.

'You mean, if they murdered Campbell. These are not men who would take on that sort of job. If they felt murderous, they'd hire someone to do the deed. But to answer your question, no, I think they'd be more discreet about their feelings if they were behind the deed.'

'So you don't think the people who talked to you are actual suspects.'

'Probably not. The ones who interest me more are the ones who didn't return my calls. Now there could be many reasons for that. They're busy men and women, with incredible demands on their time. They may get around to it yet, but their silence makes me wonder.'

'We're talking "Captains of Industry", right?' Lucy made air quotes.

Frankson smiled. 'That sort of thing, yes. And contrary to the stereotypes, most of them are decent folks, according to their lights. They didn't achieve their financial status by being hesitant to use an advantage, but none of them is the kind to "grind the faces of the poor". For the most part, I say.' He finished his pint as the waiter brought his ploughman's lunch, the biggest and most comprehensive one I've ever seen, with ham, rare roast beef, and a large slab of paté, along with two kinds of cheese, chutney, pickles, crusty bread, and various salad vegetables.

'Wow!' said Lucy. 'I might decide I'm hungry, after all.'

'I doubt I'll need dinner, if I work my way through all that. Who wants a pint, besides me?'

When that had been dealt with, and Frankson had taken

time to make some inroads into his feast, he continued. 'I said most of them are decent people. But there are two in the crowd that I wouldn't trust with bus fare. One man, one woman. They'd toss their grandmothers under that bus if they could see some profit in it. Hard as nails.' He paused to build himself a construction of bread, beef, cheddar, and chutney, and take a huge bite.

'Dagwood would be proud,' I whispered to Lucy.

'Names?' asked Alan when Frankson had swallowed.

'I'm not going to tell you. I have no wish to see any of you under a bus, and believe me, this pair would have no qualms about arranging that fate for you. What I do propose to do is to give their names and contact information to Scotland Yard and the FBI. Let them deal with the problem.'

'They may not get very far,' I said with a sigh, 'but they could at least find out if either of them was in England at the time. Passports don't lie.'

It was Frankson's turn to sigh. 'Dorothy, you haven't been listening. They wouldn't be easily traceable. Their private jets could land at almost any airstrip, with no nonsense about travel documents. But in any case, they would have hired the job done. No need to get one's own hands dirty.'

We let him finish his meal in peace.

He declined our invitation to come to the house, so we walked back alone. We didn't talk. What was there to say? Our pathways were all ending at brick walls, or sinking into bottomless mudholes.

'Maybe it was an accident, after all,' I muttered.

The others just looked at me.

Watson was reproachful when we got back. Why, his mournful countenance seemed to ask, had we gone for a walk on a lovely afternoon without him? Did we no longer love him? Had he unknowingly done something bad?

I wanted nothing more than a nap, but Lucy was game. 'Okay, old boy, go get me your leash and we'll go to the park.'

Of course Mike wanted to go, too, but we still didn't trust him outside our garden, so I scooped him up and took him up to bed with me. We were both asleep in minutes.

I was in that half-awake logy state when Watson trotted in,

back from his walk and looking for his baby. Lucy followed
him. 'I'm sorry, Aunt Dorothy. I didn't mean to wake you.'
'You didn't. I'm still asleep. This is a recording. Touch one
to disconnect.'
'I'll go away if you want, but Nigel's on the phone, and I
thought you might like to talk to him.' She held out her phone.
That woke me up. I managed to dislodge Mike, who wanted
to stay on top of his soft warm human, and slipped into my
shoes. 'Get me some tea, or coffee, will you, child? I'm still
not quite back among the living.' I took the phone. 'Nigel?
Were you able to find out anything about the Brintons?
Especially Mrs Brinton?'
'A bit. You wanted to know about her background, and if
she has money of her own, right?'
'Right.'
Lucy, bless her, put a mug of coffee in my hand and bran-
dished my notebook. I turned on the phone's speaker.
'This was so easy, you could have done it yourself.'
'Now, Nigel, you know I'm way too old to understand
computers.'
'Are not. Oh, and before I get into the details about Marilyn,
I never told you before where Brinton is from. Remember I
found his birth place and date. He was born near Edinburgh,
a little earlier than Campbell. I can't prove some of this yet,
but he got into dodgy stock dealings at an early age, and it's
reasonable to assume he was the "shadowy figure" connected
with Campbell. But anyway, about Marilyn: yes, she's inde-
pendently wealthy. Her grandfather, James Clark, was a big
noise at Marshall Field's back in the fifties and sixties. By the
way, did you know that's where Selfridge got his start? Anyway,
Clark made a lot of money and invested it well, and when he
died left it all to his only son, Marilyn's father. Who died just
under ten years ago, and Marilyn scooped the lot.'
'Interesting. Was that before or after she married Robert,
do you know?'
'Of course I know! Do you think me a stupid investigator
with no initiative? Robert and Marilyn were married exactly
a month after the will was probated.'
'Which probably took some time, as so large a sum of

money was involved. Robert was taking no chances, was he?'
Alan had joined us, bringing his cynical policeman's mind to
bear.

'Now, now,' said Nigel, 'you're making the inference that
he married her for her money. How do we know it wasn't
a flaming passion, a marriage of true lovers, a match made in
heaven?'

'We can make a pretty good guess, though. Don't forget
this guy was a pal of Iain Campbell, who wouldn't know a
flaming passion if it burnt his house down.' Lucy's tone would
have turned a swamp into the Sahara.

'Okay,' I said, 'but if he was only out for her money, what
was the attraction for her? Why did she want to marry him? Was
he doing well at that point?'

'Reasonably. I didn't have time to get deep into his finances,
but he'd been an investment banker for some time, and had
accumulated a nice pile. Nothing like her mega-millions, of
course, but nice.'

'Then . . . Nigel, when was their first child born?' Cynical
Alan again.

'Bingo! Their son was born a little more than five months
after their wedding. And was brought home to the cosy little
cottage in Sheridan Road.'

'So the house is hers.'

'Yes, another little bequest from Daddy.'

'I still don't get it,' complained Lucy. 'Okay, so she was
pregnant. But this was only seven years ago, right?'

'And a bit.'

'That's not so long ago,' Lucy went on. 'And she was rich,
and up in society's stratosphere. Why did she think they had
to marry? A generation back, yes, or in the lower classes, her
situation would have been somewhat shocking. But being
who she was, she could have pulled it off without an eyebrow
raised. Seems like there had to be some other reason.'

'We could speculate about that, of course,' said Alan a little
impatiently, 'but I don't know that it matters. We've established
that she had, and has, no need of her husband's money. If we
absolutely have to know why she married the man, we could
always have someone ask her.'

'Well, but that's just what we can't do, at least not at the moment.' Nigel paused for effect. 'That's the other thing I wanted to tell you. The lady seems to have disappeared.'

'No,' I said when we'd gone down to the parlour. 'No. I flatly and absolutely refuse to talk about it anymore. The more we learn, the less we know, and I don't intend to run around in circles forever. Unless and until we can unearth some solid evidence, the subject is closed.'

'Evidence of what?' Lucy sounded just as fed up. 'We're chasing too many ifs and maybes.'

'Exactly. I'd settle for evidence that Iain really was murdered. Or anything else! Just one provable fact in this miasma of theories! And now it's teatime, and you, Lucy, are going to make us some tea while I go next door and invite Jane to join us and bring some goodies. And we can talk of cabbages and kings, but *not* of anything remotely connected with one Iain Campbell!'

Jane had new-baked scones and a seed cake to enrich our tea. We sat in comfort around the kitchen table and chatted about nothing, fed the animals the crumbs they insisted on, and relaxed, glad to abandon our obsession for a while. Then Jane put down her cup and cleared her throat. 'Solved the mystery.'

The remark was greeted with dead silence. I don't know what my face looked like; the others were trying to look pleased, eager to hear the news, but couldn't quite bring themselves to take up the nasty subject again.

Jane was taken aback for a moment and then relaxed into a barked laugh. 'Not that mystery. Mike.'

'Oh,' I managed, trying to think what mystery there was about Mike.

'Came from London. Bought from a breeder. Hah! Kitten factory. Knows more about cash than cats. Buyer liked torties, got fed up when he saw this one was a male. Dumped him.'

'And then found out somehow that he could be valuable, and tried to get him back.' I finished the story.

Or so I thought. Jane shook her head. 'No. Breeder found out. Tried to buy him back, but buyer couldn't find him.'

'Oh, so the *breeder* was the one who tried to steal him

when he wandered away that day! I sure hope Mike scratched the daylights out of him!' said Lucy.

'*And* bit him. Might lose that hand and arm. Looks nasty,' Jane said with great relish.

'You saw him, Jane?' I inquired. 'The breeder, I mean. How did you find him?'

'Didn't. Came to me. Butter wouldn't melt. "Lost a valuable kitten. Heard you loved animals." Talked my arm off.' Another laugh. 'Gave him what for. Sent him off with a flea in his ear.'

'And told him, I trust, that you had no idea whatever what had become of his missing kitten.' Alan was wearing a broad smile.

'*And* sent the dogs after him. Wouldn't hurt a soul – but make lots of noise.'

'And he didn't know they're harmless. Jane, here's to you!' We all raised our teacups. Jane's face reddened; she hurriedly passed the seed cake.

We steadfastly kept off the subject that was occupying all our minds. If Jane wondered why, she asked no questions. Jane never pries. Unlike me, I'm sorry to say. She gathers information by osmosis, I think. Her genuine compassion, well hidden behind her brusque exterior, makes people want to confide in her. I was in fact sorely tempted to tell her all our failures to unearth anything important about Iain's death, but I restrained myself. I was pretty sure, anyway, that her response would be 'Wait'.

I'm fairly good at a number of tasks. Waiting is not one of them, but for the next couple of days I tried to close off my mind and go about my usual routine. Shopping. Church. Household chores. Walking with whoever would go with me. Napping with Mike.

Monday morning I cracked. It was close to three weeks since Iain's murder, and I couldn't turn my back on the problem anymore. Lucy was beginning to make noises about going home, and was getting increasingly frequent emails from her employer, Parkwood College. I couldn't bear the thought of sending her back with unresolved trauma hanging over her.

I found I couldn't think clearly in the house; there were too many distractions. They were all delightful, of course. People to talk to and cook for, people I loved. Animals to look after and love, animals that entertained while they demanded. I wouldn't do well as an anchorite, but I do sometimes need solitude, and this was one of those times. I helped Lucy with the breakfast dishes and then grabbed an uninteresting hat. 'I'll be back,' I said, and headed for the Cathedral.

There are many places in that vast building where one can find quiet and serenity. My favourite is the chapel reserved for private prayer. It's off the beaten path, and though people do come and go, they always respect the silence. I found a seat in the back corner, prayed for inspiration, and then just sat and let the peace take over.

We'd talked about possible suspects. Talked about motive and opportunity until we were sick of the subject. Now I turned the quest in another direction. Evidence. We needed, not ideas, but evidence. Police court evidence.

All right. What evidence could there be?

Start with the easy stuff. Fingerprints. The murder weapon, the car, was stolen. The murderer had almost certainly been smart enough to wear gloves, and the police had certainly dusted for prints on the off-chance, and found only those of the owner.

Wait a minute. Who was the owner? Was he or she a person who could have a connection, even a remote one, with one of the possible suspects?

I made a note to check that out.

Then, the car itself. Make, model, year. The car of someone wealthy, or a boring middle-class car? And . . . aha! If it was by any chance an import, with a left-hand drive, that might point to an owner from outside the UK.

Another note.

Was it possible, at this late date, to check where the car had been before it roared down Buckingham Palace Road? My heart sank at the idea. This was London I was thinking about, and one of the most congested parts of London at that. Tourists swarming nineteen to the dozen. Taxis, buses, delivery vans. The chances of one car being noticed among the tens of thousands was virtually nil.

Wait a minute, though. Congested traffic. The Congestion Charge! I'd been told that cameras, set up to enable enforcement, photographed the licence plate of every car as it entered the zone. I had no idea where the zones began and ended, but Alan would, or would know how to find out. It might be possible to trace that car, up to a point, at least.

And the Met had almost certainly thought about that.

Never mind. They couldn't think of everything. Maybe the viewpoint of a relative newcomer like me would be useful.

Newcomer. Most of our possible suspects were Americans, though not all. But if an American committed this crime, an American who didn't visit London frequently, he might not be familiar with the surveillance cameras to be found all over the place. I, who didn't visit America frequently, didn't know if they were as pervasive now in big cities in my homeland, but when I first moved to England I was appalled at seeing them on every shop, every public building, both inside and out.

So I wondered where the murderer had abandoned the car. The Met probably told Alan at the time, but I didn't remember. I wouldn't think he'd have driven it very far, so the chances were good that it was in an area under surveillance. If he'd gone straight along Buckingham Palace Road, he'd have passed the Royal Mews, along with small shops and restaurants and hotels. Then he'd have a few choices, only one of which would take him away from the cameras. A full right turn into Buckingham Gate would have taken him straight back into the world of retail. An angled right into Birdcage Walk would take him past the Guards barracks and museum. He could have chosen to circle around Queen Victoria's memorial and then gone down The Mall, with St James's Park on one side, but some important public buildings on the other.

Or, once on the circle around the memorial, he could have turned up Constitution Hill, passing between the palace gardens on one side and Green Park on the other.

Still, unless he knew London well, he might think the almost straight path into Birdcage Walk would be the safest.

So. There might be a chance that some camera, somewhere,

intended either for security surveillance or traffic control, might have picked him up as he stepped out of his car. A long shot, but possible.

Another note.

I sat in silence for a while, trying to empty my mind of all noisy thoughts, so that fresh ideas could come in.

Evidence. Anything else about the car, the weapon? Not that I could think of.

Well, then, alibis.

A dead end. Because, as Mr Frankson said, any of the possible suspects could hire someone to do the actual deed while he, the instigator, was sitting safely at home.

Wait, though. Hire. Pay. A hired killer had first to be found and then to be paid. And both those actions would have to be done discreetly. One didn't post a want ad for a hitman in the paper or online and give a credit card number.

I had no doubt that both London and Chicago offered many candidates for the job. Both the Met and the Chicago police knew who many of them were, and had informers who could tell them about more.

And how would the killer be paid? In cash, almost certainly. That would mean contact between hirer and hiree, if not directly, then through a chain.

How would I do such a thing, if I were trying to rid the world of someone I deemed undesirable?

I looked up at the cross on the altar and decided I was in a place that was unsuitable for planning a murder.

TWENTY-SIX

Though where, I wondered, would be a suitable place? Certainly nowhere in the Cathedral.

Agatha Christie and her sisters in crime planned murders routinely, probably even in their sleep. Unfortunately I couldn't ask them where they did their thinking. I knew no mystery novelists, but I certainly knew their plots.

Hundreds of them! They were all carefully laid out for me, available for the stealing, and I knew exactly where to find them.

I headed jubilantly for the public library.

Christie was probably not the best author to study. Her plots were the most ingenious in the business, but tended to rely on poison and elaborate deceptions and never, as I could remember, involved professional criminals. In fact none of my favourite authors dealt much with professional or organized crime; I much preferred the 'cosy' mystery, with clever amateur villains and detectives.

Well, then, let's see. Patricia Moyes' detective was a policeman. So was Gideon, the creation of the prolific J.J. Marric, aka John Creasey. Both those writers were long dead, though, and their books might not be available in a library. P.D. James's detective was of course a policeman, as was Ruth Rendell's best-known protagonist. Many, many of their books were on the shelves. I sighed, pulled down a few, and sat down to skim.

An hour later I was no wiser. Plenty of plots, plenty of villains, but little in the way of detailed planning of crimes, at least not the sort I needed.

I have often accused myself of being slow on the uptake, but this time my sluggish brain had outdone myself. 'Idiot!' I said aloud, winning glares from several other readers. 'Sorry, talking to myself,' I whispered as I got out of there fast.

I'd been racking my own brain, and those of superb mystery writers and their creations, when I had a true expert in crime right at home. My own husband.

The beautiful day had clouded over, and a fitful wind had sprung up, promising rain any minute. My aging legs didn't move quite fast enough, and I was pretty damp when I burst in my front door.

'Alan! Lucy! Where is everybody?'

'Here, about ready to call out the Mounties.' Lucy poked her head out the kitchen door. 'Do you realize it's well past lunchtime? Come help Alan and me put a meal together.'

'Never mind that. Alan, how would you go about hiring a killer without getting caught?'

He put down the potato he was peeling. 'I will say, conversations in this house can take the most interesting turns. Who were you planning to kill?'

'Whom. And I'm not. You are. Through an intermediary, keeping your hands nice and clean. You must have dealt with hired killers in your time.'

He resumed his chore. 'Of course, in the sense of catching them and prosecuting them. I wouldn't have cared to have any other dealings with them. They are not pleasant sorts.'

'No kidding!' Lucy drained a pot of green beans and stirred some ice cubes into them. 'We're having salade Niçoise, if you don't mind it with canned tuna. Planned while it was still a beautiful day, but I hope you think it's still okay. It'll be a while, because the potatoes have to cook and cool. Would you like a snack to tide you over?'

'What I would like,' I said in my best schoolteacher voice, 'is an answer to my question. How does one hire an assassin?'

Alan turned on the heat under the potatoes, rinsed his hands, and got some beer from the fridge. 'I take it we've resumed work on the hit-and-run case.' He sat down and poured beer for the three of us.

'Evidence. I've been doing some hard thinking about evidence, and I came up with some ideas for the police on either continent. They all have to do with the car, the murder weapon, and I imagine I'm second-guessing and all these titbits have already been examined. But then I started on alibis, even knowing that who was where on such-and-such a date is utterly irrelevant, since any of our suspects could have hired the killing done. And then I thought how hard it would be to hire a murderer without leaving a trail, and that's when I came to you. Surely you would know how it could be done. In fact, how it has in fact been done in the past.'

'You forget, my dear. When someone did it successfully, leaving no trail, we never caught up with him. He got away with it, so we'll never know just how he managed it.'

'Well, but there must have been a few cases where the villain *almost* got away with it, had *almost* the perfect plan, except something slipped up.'

'Very well. Here's the best way, in my experience. For

vehicular homicide, you need someone with nerve, but no other special skills except the ability to drive a car. So you don't have to hire a professional killer, who would be hard to find and come expensive. If I were doing it, I'd go into the seediest pub I could find and seek out a chap who seemed to be on his uppers and willing to do almost anything for a quid or two. I'd buy him a pint, and then a few more, and spin him a story about a rich gent who'd done something really awful to me. Killed my wife, assaulted my daughter, what have you. Rich enough to hire good defence lawyers, got off without even a trial.

'When the chap had enough beer to get maudlin about the injustice of it all, I'd edge around to the idea of killing him – but if I did it, they'd be sure to suspect me, because I had such a good motive. That would lead to the idea of his doing it for me. I'd make sure he thought it was his idea, and let him name an appropriate payment.

'From then on it's easy. Make all the arrangements, tell him when and where to find the victim, pay him off in cash, and vanish. The poor sap doesn't know who I am or what I look like, because I've taken care to adopt a bit of disguise. If he's caught, he can't shop me. He can't tell the police to look for the one who hated the victim for his crime, because there was no such crime. At any rate, he probably won't be caught. There are too many of his sort about. I've committed the perfect crime.'

Lucy shuddered. 'Uncle Alan, you're all too plausible. This is super scary! Are you saying this has actually happened?'

'Probably more times than we can count. There are unsolved crimes of this sort in the files of every police organization in the world. A casual crime with no motive, no connection between victim and supposed villain, gives the police no leads to follow. It's only by chance that a scheme like this can come to grief. Someone who knows both the real murderer, the pusher of the remote button, if you will, and the cat's paw, sees them together, and sees the cat's paw at the scene of the crime. If that witness happens to be an informant, he'll tell the police what he knows – for a price, of course – and that thin thread can be followed to an eventual arrest and conviction.' He got up to take the potatoes off the stove and drain them.

'You're supposing that all this,' I said, thinking hard, 'the negotiations and the crime itself, everything takes place within a certain radius in a single location, London, say. Wouldn't it be much harder to pull off if there were great distances involved?'

He dumped the potatoes in a bowl and stuck it in the freezer to cool quickly. 'Somewhat harder. Not impossible, given enough money. And it would in some ways be safer. No one on this side of the pond would be apt to recognize the actual perpetrator, and certainly no one could connect him with the button-pusher. We're talking, of course, about someone in America sending someone over here to do the deed.'

'Or hiring someone who's already here.'

Lucy's remark reverberated. A single name surfaced in both our minds.

'He didn't come to England until afterwards,' I said.

'That's what he says.' Lucy's voice was expressionless.

'Do I get the impression you're talking about Mr Frankson? I thought he was a friend,' Alan said mildly. 'Have I got the wrong end of the stick?'

'That's just it, Uncle Alan! I don't know! I thought he was a friend, too, but all I actually *know* about him is that he's given a lot of money to Parkwood College, and he's always been very pleasant to me.'

'He's got a pile of money. How did he make it? Or did he inherit it?'

'Aunt Dorothy! You sound as if just being rich is a strike against him!'

'"The rich are different from you and me". F. Scott Fitzgerald said it, and those of us who have always been in the middle class are inclined to believe it's true. We have a certain vague suspicion of the wealthy. It isn't envy, exactly, just a deep, almost subconscious feeling that they're not to be trusted.'

'I see,' said Alan. 'In England we might think it was a class distinction. Of course you don't have classes in America—'

'Don't you believe it! I'm still English, even if I did come
of age in America, and I learned fast about the classes in
America. Only they're not based on a matter of inherited titles,
like here, but things like education and money and occupation
and where a person lives. A billionaire from Harvard may or
may not rank above an equally rich numbskull who is a football
star. A struggling but highly respected lawyer in a small town
is not going to be on the A-list of anybody from New York
or LA, unless he happens to get elected to the senate, which
puts him way up there.'

'I see,' said Alan, who plainly did not. 'But we've strayed
from the point. Aside from his wealth, does either of you have
anything against Mr Frankson?'

'He didn't like Iain. Mistrusted him at first sight.'

'I'd have thought that would be a point in his favour, given
what we now know about Campbell.'

'I didn't mean it that way, exactly.' Lucy frowned. 'Yes, his
judgement was accurate, but there's the old saying, it takes
one to know one. Did he maybe just recognize a kindred
spirit?'

I pounded my empty beer glass on the table like a gavel.
'Order in the court! We're going round in circles again, dealing
with personalities instead of evidence. Let's put that salad
together and have some lunch, and then get back to real life,
to tangible evidence.'

After we ate (doling out scraps of tuna to the cats), we
gathered in the parlour for a conference. Alan took the chair,
as it were, since as a policeman he knew best what was
evidence and what was mere conjecture.

'Very well. Let's dispose first of Mr Frankson. What
evidence do we have, or might we find, indicating his guilt?'

I thought hard. 'His passport would show when he came
to England.'

'Irrelevant. As we've been discussing, he has the where-
withal to hire someone to do the actual deed.'

'We could check up on his English cronies, see if he knows
anyone here who could have been bribed to drive the car, or
find someone else to do it.' Lucy didn't sound very hopeful.

'Too risky, and unlikely,' Alan pronounced. 'If said "crony" is a dependable friend, he'd be most unlikely to pass as a lowlife in a pub. If he's undependable, he might give under pressure and lead the police back to Frankson. No, I can't see him hiring anyone here. I suppose he could have done it from the American end.'

'But how?' I ran my fingers through my hair. 'That seems even less likely. You've met him. Can you imagine him even knowing about the kind of place where you could hire a petty criminal? Much less passing as a customer? He looks and acts and sounds exactly like what he is, a successful and wealthy businessman. I can see him losing his temper with somebody and pasting him one, but not planning an elaborate murder scheme. Lucy?'

'I think you're right on. Plus, we don't know of any reason why he might want Iain dead, even if he didn't like him. I think we can wash out Fred Frankson.'

'That being the object of the exercise, we'll drop him and carry on with our pursuit of evidence. Dorothy, love, did your solitary meditation yield anything we can take to court?'

'Not yet, but I did come up with a few ideas. Mind you, the various police entities have probably already followed it all up, but here goes.'

TWENTY-SEVEN

I settled myself with the cup of tea Lucy had thoughtfully brewed, and took out my notebook. Emmy observed the signs that I was going to stay put for a while and dived into my lap, with a look that dared me to try to move her. I used her back as a book rest and began.

'I thought first about the murder weapon, the car. We know it was stolen, and of course I'm sure the police have examined it thoroughly for fingerprints and any other possible clues to the driver. But it occurred to me that the car itself might be traced, using the Congestion Zone traffic cameras.'

'But we know who owns the car, Dorothy. The Met looked into that thoroughly. He works as a guide at Apsley House, and normally leaves his car at home in Cheam. However, on the day in question, he drove into London because he had a meeting in Brentwood not long after the end of his work day, and the train connections didn't fit with the timing. So he drove in very early in the day, so as to be able to park in the very limited space available. The house, Dorothy, is the home of the current Duke of Wellington, but also a museum in honour of the first duke, the one who defeated Napoleon at Waterloo. It stands square in the middle of London, at Hyde Park Corner, so you can imagine the parking situation. When he came out to go to his meeting, the car was gone. Incidentally, the poor chap missed his meeting.'

I digested that. 'Where's Cheam? And Brentwood?'

'At opposite compass points from London. Cheam is south-west, Brentwood northeast. Both pleasant, affluent suburbs. Easy journeys by train, but slow, late in the afternoon. The train to Brentwood leaves from Liverpool Street, and there are unfortunately a number of changes of Tube lines to get there from Hyde Park Corner.'

'But would a car do any better, at the height of rush hour? I just can't understand why anyone who knew London would choose to drive. I've never fought London traffic, thank the Lord, but Frank and I got caught once or twice in Chicago at rush hour—'

'Which in Chicago is twenty-four-seven,' Lucy interjected.

'—so I can imagine what it's like. It would take that man ages just to get out of London onto a main road, and even then he'd be braving all the other commuters eager to get home. It makes no sense.'

'Hmm.' Alan tented his fingers and pursed his lips in thought. 'You have a point, my dear. I don't know that the Met thought about that. They verified the ownership of the car and the owner's bona fides and apparently left it at that. They did say he's a respectable fellow, retired from an architectural firm, keen on houses of historical value, hence his interest in Apsley House. He's even on their board of trustees.'

'I don't care how respectable he is,' snapped Lucy. 'I thought Iain was, too. The whole set-up smells. Isn't it just a tad too convenient that this car just happened to be available, when it usually wouldn't be? Not too far from Victoria Station, either. And why on earth would Mr Respectable get himself into a meeting at that time of day, anyway, when he knew getting there on time would be almost impossible? What I want to know is, does this history buff have any connection with somebody who hated Iain?'

Alan nodded thoughtfully. 'Looks as though there are several things the Met needs to find out about this squeaky-clean citizen. Dorothy, what other nuggets have you dug out of that fertile criminal brain of yours?'

'Well, I've thought of another possible trap for our villain. Those congestion cameras aren't the only ones recording everything that happens. Surveillance cameras are absolutely everywhere in London. When I first moved to England, I didn't even know what CCTV stood for, but when I learned about closed-circuit television, I was appalled at how little privacy there was. Maybe it's gotten bad back home now, but meanwhile it's terrible here. Every shop has one, every public building. For all I know, every cop on the beat has a body cam. In London, anyway, you can't move without having your picture taken.

'Now. When the car hit Iain, it was headed up Buckingham Palace Road. If it stayed on that path, there would be shops and hotels and public buildings thick as blackberries in July. No matter which way the driver turned, he'd be observed by some camera or other. And I don't think he'd turn. I think he'd go on as straight as he could until he got past the palace and away from the thickest traffic, and then find a spot to ditch the car. Where was it found, Alan?'

'One of those byways off Parliament Square, parked illegally half on the pavement. It was obstructing a pub's cellar access, so the publican saw it almost immediately and was rather annoyed.'

Breathing fire, I translated. 'I hope the pub has CCTV.'

'Of course. Out of order at the time, however.'

I rolled my eyes. 'Just our luck. But you said the owner

saw the car right away. I wonder if there was a passer-by who saw the guy get out of the car.'

'Probably, since he parked in a way that would draw attention. And how many people were in that vicinity at that time, would you say?'

'In the centre of the tourist mecca of London on an April afternoon. Right. The place would be packed, even though the weather was awful. That makes it worse, actually. Everyone would have been sporting umbrellas and hurrying to get where they were going.' I sighed and held up my hands in surrender. 'So unless the witness was a regular at the pub, and talked about the incident, we've struck out there.'

'Not necessarily. The killer would have been driving slowly. For one thing, he was looking for a place to get rid of the car, and in that quarter of London they're thin on the ground. And the traffic in those parts always moves at a crawl.'

'I've always thought,' said Lucy, 'that anyone who drives a bus or a cab in London, or Chicago or New York, for that matter, is completely bonkers. If he wasn't already when he started on the job, he would be soon. Sorry, Uncle Alan. I interrupted.'

'I agree, though. Just think about trying to get an emergency vehicle through those streets, an ambulance or firetruck. Or even worse, imagine being in need of such assistance and waiting as precious minutes go by. However, we digress. The point I was going to make is that the killer almost certainly had to stop from time to time, and in that area of great density, there may well be a picture of the car and driver somewhere. The problem there, though, is the quality of the photos. Even when the subject is close to the camera, the image is often unsatisfactory. From a few metres away . . .' He shook his head. 'Still, it's worth looking into, along with your other suggestions. Anything else?'

'No, I'm thunk out, at least until the Met gets anything useful from what you tell them. Lucy, is there any more tea?'

'I'm afraid not. I can make some. Or how would you like to take a walk with me and Watson? It's only drizzling. And when we come back we can have a little stronger stuff.'

So we whiled away the rest of the day pleasantly, and I went to sleep that night thinking about what I was going to ask Bob Finch to plant in that bare spot in my back garden.

In the morning I forgot about gardening. The drizzle from yesterday had turned into a steady downpour. The old saying about waiting a minute for a change in the weather used to apply to southern Indiana, and certainly does to southern England. Today, though, I was pretty sure that it would take far more than a minute for the rain to change to something pleasant. I was very tempted to scrunch back under the covers and laze away the day, but I knew I'd only ruin my sleep rhythms for the next day or two. So, grumbling, I heaved myself out of bed.

It seemed I was the first one up, because all the animals were lurking outside the bedroom door waiting for human service. This time, before letting Watson out, I had a towel at the ready to dry him off before he could spray rainwater all over me. I ignored the cats' complaints about the rain that I had plainly conjured up just to annoy them, and gave them extra treats to make up for the weather.

The smell of brewing coffee (surely one of the finest perfumes in the universe) roused the rest of the family, and over breakfast we discussed plans for the day. Alan was anticipating calls from Scotland Yard in reply to the suggestions he'd sent. Lucy debated whether to call Frankson or not, and I decided to wait and see what developed, meanwhile making one of my old American standby meals for a nasty day, chilli.

The best-laid plans, as someone almost said, can be knocked for a loop. I did get the chilli put together and it was simmering nicely when Alan walked into the kitchen looking important.

'Where's Lucy? She should hear this.'

She came into the room carrying Mike, who had decided he didn't want to be shooed away.

'I've been talking to the Met,' he began. *Well, we knew that!* 'They had been following up on a matter we never even thought about.'

He waited for us to question him. Even in the short time

she'd spent with us, Lucy had learned that it was best to ignore his provoking delays. He'd get to the point quicker if we stayed silent.

He grinned. 'You're onto me, both of you. All right, here it is. None of us wondered about exactly how the murderous car got stolen. It isn't easy these days, you know. A thief can't just hotwire the ignition of a late-model car, because anything built in the last ten or fifteen years has no key slot. No ignition key, in fact. Everything is computer controlled and works with the key fob.'

Lucy, who had probably never heard the term 'hotwire', looked puzzled.

'Get Alan to explain later, dear,' I said. 'Alan, I thought there were ways to steal information from a fob.'

'To hack it, in other words. There are ways, of course. Every time engineers design new and better security systems, crooks devise new and better ways to get around them. If a thief can get close to the fob, he can use a device to hack it, transfer its codes to almost anything – his mobile, perhaps – and Bob's your uncle.

'But that means, as I said, the thief getting near enough, within a few metres, to use the hacking device. The far easier way, and the way hundreds of cars are stolen every day in the UK, is simply to get in and drive it away. And before you ask how that's possible, the answer is idiotically simple. The key fob has been left in the car.'

'You can't mean people actually leave their keys in the car!'

'They do. A lot more often than they used to, actually. Back when everything was done with an ignition key, one had to turn the key to turn off the engine, and it was instinctive to pull the key out and put it in a pocket. In any case, one's house key was often on the same chain.

'Now, a touch turns off the engine. There's no key to think about. Some people, believe it or not, leave the fob in the glove compartment all the time.'

'But – but you can't even lock the car with the fob inside!' I was babbling.

'I said the matter was idiotically simple. Emphasis on the adverb.'

'So that's what happened?' Lucy was sceptical. 'Mr Respectable left his key fob in the unlocked car? In London?'

'He did. It was still in the car when it was found.'

'And we're meant to believe that he did this accidentally?' I echoed Lucy. 'Right. His mind was on other things. He never did such a thing ordinarily.'

'Sarcasm, my dear, is the tool of the devil, as you so frequently point out to me. That was, indeed, his original story. It may change, now that the police are questioning him more closely. They're quite interested in any connections, however tenuous, with Mr Campbell.'

'I should think so! Are we maybe getting somewhere at last?'

'It seems possible. Now, whatever is bubbling away in that pot smells tantalizing. Is it perhaps almost ready?'

I put together some cornbread to go with my utterly American meal, and it had just come out of the oven when Lucy's phone rang.

'Drat! It's Fred, and he's going to want to talk and talk, and I'm hungry. Maybe I won't answer.'

But, like me, she found it impossible to ignore a ringing phone. 'Hello?' It wasn't a welcoming greeting.

'Lucy, Fred. I realize this may not be the best time, but I'm in Sherebury and I have some news. May I come to see you?'

She put a hand over the phone and said, 'He wants to come over. Says he has news.'

I sighed and said, 'Invite him to lunch. I hope he can eat peasant food.'

'We're about to sit down to lunch. Aunt Dorothy's made chilli, if you'd like to join us.'

'Tell her I love chilli and I'll be there in five minutes.'

He made it in three, apologizing profusely for the intrusion. 'But I thought you'd want to hear about this right away.'

'Yes, but surely it can wait for a few minutes. Chilli improves the longer it sits, but cornbread does not. Have a seat, everybody.'

Frankson was too much of a gentleman to wolf his food, exactly, but it was clear he wasn't tasting anything he ate. He contributed almost nothing to the table conversation, so eager was he to get all this nourishment nonsense out of the way and impart his news. Finally I took pity on him, served coffee and some chocolate biscuits, and said, 'All right. We appreciate your patience. What did you want to tell us?'

'Two things. One is simply negative information. That is, solid information that actually puts us a step back. The Met has looked into the recent activities of my two best suspects, and unfortunately they could not have had anything to do with Campbell's death. They took off for the Cayman Islands about a month ago. Together, I might add, though they both had spouses at home.'

'Well, but it's not their morals we're concerned about,' I said, rather annoyed. 'And they could as easily hire a hitman from the Caymans as from anywhere else.'

'Quite right. They could have. Unfortunately one of those deserted spouses apparently took umbrage at this latest infidelity, and got the idea of an arranged "accident" himself. The two travelled from their homes in New York directly to Grand Cayman in his private jet. The plane had been tampered with and crashed into the Mediterranean a few minutes before the scheduled landing. All aboard were killed.'

I couldn't find anything to say.

Eventually Alan cleared his throat. 'You said you had something else to tell us.'

'Yes. Not great news, but at least this bit gets us one step ahead instead of back. The police working on the case on my side of the pond finally found Marilyn Brinton. She'd been at home the whole time; just not answering the phone or the doorbell. Anyway, they got her to tell them where her husband was. Sort of. Don't get all excited, though. Under pressure, she admitted that he had gone to London to meet with Campbell, a day or two before the death. She swore that he couldn't possibly have had anything to do with it, that he would never do a thing like that, yada, yada, yada. She was most reluctant to say any more, and claimed she hadn't heard from him in days, but eventually parted grudgingly with the information that Robert usually stays at the Hilton when he's in London.'

'The Hilton!' I waved it away. 'That's a nice enough hotel,

certainly, but surely with all his money he'd prefer something a little more luxurious, a little more English. Claridge's, the Ritz, the Dorchester, Brown's—'

'Yes, he could probably afford any of those, but Mrs Brinton said he prefers "good American service". The cop I talked to said he got the impression that Robert, or more likely Marilyn, was somewhat tightfisted and not apt to throw money away on fancy European frills.'

'Right.' Alan wasn't interested in Brinton's views about luxury. 'So he's at the Hilton. I presume the Met has gone to talk to him.'

'They would certainly have liked to do that.' Frankson's voice was very dry. 'He isn't there. He hasn't been there. He hasn't tried to register there. They've heard nothing from him since his last stay, almost a year ago. The management has no idea where he is. Neither, apparently, has Mrs Brinton. This time the American cops think she's telling the truth.'

TWENTY-EIGHT

'Passport Control.' When Alan becomes terse, he's in full police mode.

'Been checked,' Frankson replied, just as tersely. 'Unless he's pulled a fast one, he's still in England.'

'So he's in trouble. I don't . . . I certainly don't think very kindly of him, but honestly, I don't know if I can take another death!' Lucy's voice wobbled and Watson wormed himself under the table to sit on her feet.

'In trouble, or in hiding,' said Alan calmly. 'Or both. Certainly he's in trouble from the point of view of the police. We . . . they aren't too happy with people who deliberately avoid them. Can we think of some reason he'd be hiding from anyone except the law?'

'If he didn't order Campbell killed,' I answered, 'the people, or person, who did, could be after Brinton, too. For the same reasons.'

'Yes, Aunt Dorothy, but we haven't been able to track any of them down.' She didn't add 'so that's no help' but I got the gist.

'I know. I offered the suggestion for what it's worth, but what I really suspect is that he's hiding from his wife. Mr Frankson—'

'Fred.'

'Fred, you said the Chicago cops, or whoever talked to Mrs Brinton, thought she was telling the truth this time when she said she didn't know where Robert was. I know it's hard to get an impression second-hand, but did you get any idea of what her attitude was? I mean, she's been stonewalling all this time and then gave in – and then he's not at the Hilton after all. So what's going on in her mind?'

'As you say, Mrs Martin—'

'Dorothy. Only fair, if you're Fred.'

He smiled. It was a sweet smile that transformed the rather formidable big-deal businessman into a warm human being. 'Dorothy, then – as you say, it's hard to catch nuances second-hand. But this man struck me as having a pretty keen understanding of human nature, and what he actually said was that he'd swear Mrs Brinton was dumbfounded when she heard Robert couldn't be located. "Lost her cool there for minute" were his actual words.'

'Hmm. "Lost her cool" as in "sounded afraid about her husband", or as in "lost her temper"?'

But Fred couldn't tell us that. 'I suppose I could call her myself,' he said dubiously.

'What excuse would you have for that? You don't know her, do you?'

'Never met her in my life. I've heard of her, of course. The *Trib* ran a story about her father's death and her inheritance. It was a big deal because of the Marshall Field connection. If there was a notice about her marriage to Brinton, I missed it. Probably ran only in the local paper. The *Trib* doesn't go in for society news much.'

'Then I don't see how you could call her, without making her very suspicious. The cops have already been at her, at least twice, and she's been pretty cagey with them, at least until

was sure this woman knew more than she was telling. That information could be valuable. Fred was right.

Alan's face told me he didn't much like it either, but he sighed and got out his phone. 'I'll let the Met know. At this point, proper procedure is called for, I think.'

So we waited for the mills of bureaucracy to grind as slowly as usual. Lucy and I took Watson for a walk. Fred hung around for a while, restless, impatient with Alan's caution, before finally taking off. I thought about starting something for dinner, but after staring at the contents of the freezer for several minutes without seeing a thing, gave it up as a bad job. When we got hungry, we could go out somewhere or send for carryout.

Alan's phone rang just before I got to the nail-biting stage. The call was brief. He clicked off and gave us the news.

'Marilyn Brinton has flown. Her house is closed up. Her security people say she told them she'd be away for several days. The police found out who her childminder is; she has the children at her house and said the same thing, that Mrs Brinton couldn't say for sure when she'd be back.'

'And no one knows where she's gone?'

'She didn't tell anyone directly, but the minder heard her tell the little boy she'd bring him a teddy bear if he was good. Quote "dressed up like one of the Queen's guards".'

'So . . . London!'

'England, anyway. Airports have been alerted.'

TWENTY-NINE

We ended up going to the Rose and Crown, where Fred insisted on treating us to dinner. I felt awkward about it, since it was our idea, but he gave me a lecture.

'Look here, Dorothy. I understand and appreciate your point of view. But the fact is that I'm the one imposing on you. I've been taking up your time, as an uninvited guest. Besides which,

I am, as some people would say, filthy rich. It not only gives me pleasure to repay your good nature, but it's fun to spend money enjoying myself. Deal?'

'Deal. With the understanding that *I'm* going to make *you* a lovely meal one of these days.'

We solemnly shook hands to seal the agreement, and sat down to our dinner basking in good will. 'I hope you don't mind,' said Alan as we savoured our pre-prandial drinks, 'but I want to keep my phone in my pocket. I know it's rude, over a meal, but I think we all want to know when they pick up Mrs Brinton.'

We agreed heartily, and kept an ear open all through three delightful courses, but the phone was obstinately silent.

We went back to the house for coffee, and worried. 'Let's see. I called her around ten, her time. If she decided to head across the Atlantic right then, it would still take her at least a couple of hours to pack and get to O'Hare.'

'Would it have to be O'Hare?' asked Lucy.

'I don't know. Does Midway have any international flights?'

'To Canada and Mexico, I think. I don't know about transatlantic.'

'Any international airport, no matter how limited, can deal with private flights to virtually any destination,' put in Fred. 'Chicago to London needs a runway long enough to accommodate a plane with a fairly heavy load. All that fuel weighs a lot, you know. If I were going to do it, I'd fly from O'Hare. Long runways, and a big selection of jets for hire. But on the whole, if she could find a seat on a commercial flight, it would probably be quicker. Unless you own your own jet, or are associated with a company that does, you can't just hop on, you know. Arrangements have to be made, and a flight plan filed, and these things take time. I take it you're trying to work out how soon she could land on British soil.'

'Yes, and you're quite right,' said Alan handsomely. 'Knowing nothing about the private jet set, I was vastly underestimating. If she had to fly commercial, it would arrive . . . when?'

'All the flights out of Chicago that I know about,' I said, 'are red-eyes. They leave after dinner sometime and get to

London at some painfully early hour the next morning. Frank and I used to fly that way, and we'd be wiped out for the next couple of days. And you remember, Alan, that flight back from Indiana a few years ago? And the one from Toronto?'

'How could I have forgotten! Yes, not an ideal schedule. So I needn't have brought my phone to dinner after all.'

'I'd say we won't hear anything till early tomorrow morning.' Fred waggled one hand in the equivocating gesture. 'But you never know. If all the stars aligned for her, she could land somewhere in the middle of the night. I fear you may not get too much sleep tonight.'

He was right about that. We went up early after a long and wearisome day, and I kept going over and over in my mind what we knew and what we suspected about the murder of Iain Campbell.

We knew Iain was a con man who had left behind him a string of disgruntled victims of his frauds. Some, those who had been bilked of larger sums than most, were more than disgruntled. If one of them had been furious enough to kill him, or have him killed, we were apparently no nearer to knowing who.

We knew that Iain was a Scot who had been associated for some time with an American named Robert Brinton, and had even gone so far as to enter into marriage with him, a marriage that was as fraudulent as most of Iain's ventures, for Robert had a wife and two children back home. Presumably Iain didn't know that, so the charge of fraud should be laid at Robert's door. If Iain had some nefarious legal scheme in mind with the marriage, it wouldn't have worked. Could the idea have been Robert's? For some equally twisted reason? We had all got to the point that we wouldn't have believed a sworn statement from either of them to the effect that the earth was round.

And then there was Mrs Brinton, Robert's real spouse. Two children, one conceived well before the marriage. I was old enough, and still hidebound enough, to view that detail with some disapproval. Which was ridiculous, and had, as W.S. Gilbert might have said, nothing to do with the case.

But she had been less than truthful with the police when

they were searching for Robert, first claiming she didn't know, and then giving them false information.

I squirmed uncomfortably, turning to my other side, trying not to disturb Alan. Because I was pretty sure Mrs Brinton's most recent statement to the police wasn't a deliberate lie. She told them where she thought Robert was, and was flummoxed when she found out he wasn't there. Now she had taken off for England. To try to find him? To make sure that the police *didn't* find him? And did all of this have anything to do with Iain's death? Should we be concentrating on some of the other tangled threads, like perhaps the owner of the murder car?

I turned over again. Alan grunted.

'Sorry, love.'

'Not to worry. I can't sleep, either.'

Our favourite cure for a spot of sleeplessness wasn't going to work tonight. Neither of us was in the mood.

'Do you think they'll be able to stop her when her plane lands?'

'At a major airport, yes. If she's flying privately and lands at a small airfield, the odds get much worse.'

'But every airfield has to follow the same rules, surely.'

'Our trouble, Dorothy, yours and mine, is that we assume the laws will be obeyed. Yes, the rules are the same for all. Some choose to ignore them.'

'Oh.'

'And we think we're dealing with one of the rule breakers.'

Somehow talking about it had lulled me almost asleep, when Alan's phone rang, sounding in the quiet of the night like a disaster siren. He swiped to answer and turned on the light. 'Yes. Where? Ah. I see. Right.'

I didn't have to ask.

'Private plane, landed at Heathrow. The Met didn't detain her, but are following her, hoping she'll lead them to her husband.'

I yawned, the tension now relieved. 'What time is it?'

'Almost four thirty. Go back to sleep. Nothing more will happen till morning, if then.'

He put a comforting arm around me and we were both asleep in minutes.

* * *

Morning came all too soon, of course. I finally surfaced to the smell of coffee and low-voiced conversation. Alan had thoughtfully closed the bedroom door when he went down, so I wasn't greeted by a happy, lively cat. I pushed my feet into slippers and my arms into the sleeves of a robe and sleepwalked down to the kitchen.

No one said a word to me until I was well into my second cup of coffee. Then Alan grinned. 'Back among the living?'

'Sort of. Do I remember that Mrs Brinton got to England in the middle of the night?'

'You do, and there have been developments. How do you want your eggs?'

'Later. Just toast for now. What developments?'

He sat down with his own coffee while Lucy popped my favourite wholemeal bread into the toaster. 'We thought, anyway the Met thought, that the lady would head straight for the Hilton. Not a bit of it. Instead she gave the cabbie an address in . . . guess.'

'Have a heart, Alan! I'm operating on about three hours of sleep.'

'Sorry, love. But when I tell you you'll be a lot more alert. Mrs Robert Brinton is now in the London suburb of Cheam, at the home of the man we've been calling Mr Respectable.'

'The owner of the car!'

'Exactly. Here's your toast.'

'The circle closes.' I don't know if I meant to sound menacing, but it came across that way. Lucy shuddered.

'Not quite yet,' said Alan, 'but it's certainly narrowing. Mrs Robert Brinton will have some explaining to do, as will Mr Respectable Charles Crane.'

'I suppose Robert Brinton is there, too, so the Met can round them all up in one swell foop.'

'They hoped so, too, and so, I imagine, did his wife, but he is not. It begins to look as though she is genuinely in the dark about his movements.'

'But she came here – to England, I mean – to look for him. So she thinks he's still in this country.'

'Looks that way, doesn't it?' Fred Frankson walked into

the kitchen. 'I did knock, but you were all too busy talking to hear. I gather things are happening.'

Alan brought him up to date while Lucy fried bacon and scrambled enough eggs to feed us all.

'Ah. Mrs Brinton was unwise to visit Mr . . . Crane, did you say?'

'She was,' said Alan, shaking his head. 'That was a connection she certainly didn't want to reveal. It shows, I think, just how disturbed she is by Robert's disappearance.'

We were thinking about that, and devouring our meal, when Lucy's phone rang. She swiped it. 'Hello?'

She listened for an instant while looking at the caller ID. 'No, this is Lucy Bowman. Who's calling, please?' She then mouthed to us, *Chicago area*.

I gestured, and she turned on the speaker. 'Oh, I think you should certainly recognize my voice, considering how long we talked yesterday. You seem to have lost your southern accent, though. Have a lovely day, whoever you are. And wherever you are.' The caller clicked off.

'Uh-oh.' It seemed the only thing to say.

'Lucy,' Alan asked urgently, 'who knows you're staying with us?'

'Tons of people. Everyone at the university, of course. I mean everyone I dealt with, but it's a small place and I was sort of a visiting celebrity. Most people there know, I'd guess. And of course your friends here. And the couple who've gone to India: Penny and Colin whatever. And Carrie and her husband.' She held up her hands in a gesture of helplessness.

'And back in the States?'

'I told the people I work with. I had to give them an emergency phone number, in case something happened to my cell. Mobile. And . . . Iain.'

'And if Iain knew,' I said wearily, 'he might well have told Brinton. Using your phone seemed like a brilliant idea, Lucy, but it's backfired. Probably the whole gang of them know where to find me now.'

'That might be a good thing,' said Fred with a thoughtful smile. 'We could get the minions of the law here to watch for them if they come—'

'With Dorothy as tethered goat?' Alan's voice was one I'd never before heard from him. It would have frozen boiling water in the jungle.

Fred looked at him in surprise, and then spread his hands. 'Sorry. Stupid idea. Forgive me.'

Lucy looked shocked. I tried to smile, but the thought had shaken me. I've walked straight into dangerous situations in my life, but almost always when I hadn't realized how dangerous they might be. To sit and wait for somebody to come and attack me . . .? No, thank you.

'Wait a minute. Why should Mrs Brinton come here? Okay, so now she's figured out that somebody called from here, using Lucy's phone, and found out a lot about her. But what does that matter? She's probably clever enough to realize that she told me a lot more than she said in words. So what? Why should she care that someone knows about her none-too cordial relationship with her husband?'

'Follow it through, Dorothy. She's the wife of Robert Brinton, the one-time partner of Iain Campbell. She almost certainly knows that Iain was deeply involved with Lucy Bowman, and could easily have learned where Lucy is just now. She knows that the police are very eager to learn who murdered Iain. You reckon her to be an intelligent woman. It doesn't take much of a stretch for her to assume that the strange woman who called to pick her brains, on a very flimsy excuse, is connected to Lucy, is near enough to her to borrow her phone, and might well be working for the police. Do you agree that she might want to have a little chat with you?'

'Oh.' I gestured helplessly. 'I guess I'm still not firing on all cylinders. Maybe I need to go back up for a nap.'

'You do that. Meanwhile I'm going to get back to the Met and see what's going on in Cheam.'

This time I was glad of the comforting presence of Mike and Watson. Mike curled up next to me, with Watson on the floor. Mike purred, Watson snored. The lullaby sent me straight off.

THIRTY

I don't know how long I slept, but when I woke, feeling much more like myself, the house was very quiet and my furry attendants were gone. I showered and dressed and went downstairs in search of someone to talk to.

I could find no one but a pair of sleepy cats, who looked up from their repose in a patch of sunshine, yawned, stretched, and went back to sleep. So much for loving companions.

There didn't seem to be any other life forms around the house or in the garden. It was well after lunchtime, so they all must have eaten, not wanting to disturb me, and gone out somewhere. Well, darn it, I was hungry. I wandered into the kitchen and checked the fridge for sandwich material.

It was full of cold meat and cheese and salad. Plenty for lunch for several people. Nothing much seemed to be missing, so I wondered what the rest had scrounged. Blast, if they'd gone out to eat without me, they were going to hear about it.

I made myself a sandwich, poured some tonic, added a chunk of lime that had seen better days, and sat down without much enthusiasm to eat it.

I like company with my meals. Alan and I rub along very nicely together, but of late, Lucy had added a brightness to our conversation, a sparkle to the air. Little Mike, of course, was always good for some entertainment. Drat it all, where *was* everyone? I missed them. Even Sam and Emmy were too sound asleep to come in search of a handout.

I put down my sandwich. This was silly. A few years ago I would have had to wait impatiently for someone to turn up. Now in these days of instant communication, I had but to lift my phone. If I could find it.

Usually when I lost my phone, I could ask Alan to call me, or use the landline. We gave up our landline a while back, and it was Alan I was trying to locate, so I simply had to in store for me.' Her voice gave out. She finished her bourbon at a gulp.

'But no,' Alan went on, 'it doesn't look as though Robert killed Iain, or arranged for him to be killed. There hasn't been time to question him thoroughly, of course, but he insists he had no part in the matter.'

'And you believe him?' Fred sounded extremely sceptical.

'The people from the Met are inclined to believe him, yes. You must remember, Mr Frankson, that they are highly trained in interrogation techniques.'

It was a very polite slap-down, but Fred recognized it as such.

'Sorry, sorry. The cops in America aren't always . . . well, anyway, I stand reproved.' He raised his glass in an apologetic salute, and Alan murmured something noncommittal.

'Do go on with the story,' Inga prompted. 'Robert Brinton recognized you.'

'Recognized Lucy, at any rate. He hadn't expected her to be accompanied by so many companions. Unfortunately I was holding Watson's leash, and he had led me to the door of the butcher shop. Unfortunately, because it meant Lucy was closest to the kerb.'

'So he just opened the passenger door and reached out and grabbed me,' she said. 'I was too startled to resist much, but I must have screamed. And then things got very complicated.'

'Watson,' I conjectured.

'Exactly,' said Alan. 'He's an old dog, but you know how protective he is with those he loves. And here were two of his friends in trouble, not only Lucy, but Mike, his beloved child. He tore the leash out of my hand and was in the car before Brinton had time to move more than a foot or two.'

'That's when he bit him,' said Lucy with great satisfaction. 'Jumped right over me and bit him on the leg. Hard. Dear little Bob wasn't a happy camper. It's a good thing our sweet little Mike doesn't speak Human. Bob's reaction wasn't fit for the ears of a baby.'

'The car took off with a roar,' Alan continued, 'and there

was no way I could keep up. To make matters worse, Watson had knocked me down with his energetic action, and when I got up I found I'd fallen on my phone. I think it's beyond repair.'

'That must have been when I started wondering where everyone was, and tried to call you.'

'Probably. At any rate, I couldn't phone the police, so I hobbled into the butcher shop and used their phone. I'm ashamed to say I'd been so startled I neglected to notice the licence number, though I could describe the car. And you know how many byways there are turning off the High Street, especially once you get past the Cathedral. So it seemed like a futile pursuit, and I was getting more and more agitated.'

'But by that time,' Lucy picked up the story, 'Mike had gone into action. He didn't like being grabbed. He didn't like being driven fast and bounced around in a car. And especially he didn't like it that I was unhappy. So he went to work. Just jumped right on the creep and dug in his claws. First his arm, and then on up to his face. Kitten claws are very sharp, and Robert foolishly tried to push him away. The claws held on. Blood was getting into the guy's eyes, and he was in pain, and so he lost control of the car. And that, darling Aunt Dorothy, is where you came in.'

I sighed. 'And very glad I did, too. Oh, did you try to call me at some point?'

'Oh, I forgot. That was just before Mike started his attack. I grabbed my phone and hit your number, but the creep slammed it away, and I couldn't find it until he crashed the car. It still works, but it doesn't look too great.' She showed up the badly cracked glass. 'Oh, well, if that's my only casualty, I count myself lucky.'

'Speaking of casualties,' said Fred, 'I assume the crook wasn't badly hurt, if the cops were able to question him.'

'Not badly. His head hit the steering wheel and knocked him out for a little while, but the most serious damage was inflicted by that innocent baby there.' He pointed to Mike, who was now stretched out in deep slumber. 'I'm told his face may never be the same, and the doctors are he has refused to answer any questions about that incident, I believe these police officers wish to ask if you can shed any light on the matter.'

'Who says he was trying to abduct anyone? He was just—'

'I say so. I was a witness to the acts. I have told the officers here exactly what I saw, and Miss Bowman has added her testimony. There is really no question about what happened. The only remaining question is his motivation for such an idiotic crime.'

It must have been that word that did it. Mrs Brinton leapt to her feet. The constable moved up, but Mrs Brinton shrieked and shook her off. 'Idiotic! Idiotic! I'll say it was idiotic. Just like everything else that boob has done in this whole crock! So simple, he said. Get rid of Campbell and the money's all ours. Simple! Then little Miss Bright-Eyes here has to go and stay with a big-noise cop, and they smell a rat and start turning over rocks.'

She paused for breath, and the inspector said, 'Mrs Brinton, I must caution you that you are being recorded. You do not have to say anything, but—'

She screamed over his words. 'I'll say what I damn well please! It's all your fault, sweetie pie! You couldn't keep your mouth shut, could you? I'd like to shut it for you—'

She lunged at Lucy, and it took the combined efforts of Alan, the inspector, and the amazingly strong little constable to subdue her.

THIRTY-TWO

Quite a large party was gathered in our parlour a week later. I felt very safe in the presence of two officers from Scotland Yard and three from our local force. Almost all of our best friends were there: Jane; the Endicotts; Nigel (Greta staying behind to look after the kids); the dean and his wife. Lucy had delayed her return to the States, and had invited Fred to join the group.

It was a mid-afternoon gathering, to accommodate the inn-keepers' work schedule, and on a perfectly beautiful day we overflowed into the back garden. Drinks focussed on tea and lemonade and an occasional beer, and Jane had brought over a huge platter of ham and cheese and homemade bread, and we were a merry group.

We had gathered for two reasons: to hear the end of the story, and to honour Mike. Mike, however, in view of the size of the crowd, had chosen to remove himself to sanctuary under the sofa, so we had to drink to him *in absentia*.

'So here's to a brave defender of the innocent, and of the law,' said Alan, hoisting a cup of tea.

'And this is probably the time to tell you,' said the inspector, 'that we're having a badge made for him. He's been sworn in officially as a deputy. Without him, and Watson of course, Brinton might have got away with it.'

We all applauded, and Alan said, 'I suggest you all sit down, because we have quite a story to tell you. Dorothy, my dear, will you do the honours?'

'I'll begin, but I'll need a lot of help from our stalwart police. But actually, it's hard to know where to begin, because there's such a knot to untangle.'

'Start with the Brintons, Aunt Dorothy.'

I nodded. 'You're probably right, because it does begin – and end – with them.' I took a sip of lemonade. 'I'll try not to get too tedious, but the character of Marilyn Brinton is the key. No . . . mixed metaphor. Is the critical thread that launched . . . no.' Laughter. 'All right, forget the images. Marilyn Clark grew up surrounded by affluence, and in her case it led to avarice. She had, one would think, all the material goods that anyone could want, especially after inheriting her grandfather's fortune. But it was never enough. We had assumed that Robert Brinton married her for her money. In fact, it seems it was the other way round.'

'Is this just surmise, Dorothy?' asked Peter.

'No. I had a long conversation with Marilyn last week when she calmed down a bit. Apparently my authoritarian school-teacher persona broke right through her defences. At any rate, she told me the story of her life. The *Cliff Notes* version is that the poor little rich girl was starved for love, and as often happens, she sought it in the wrong way. She came across Robert Brinton through some business dealings—'

'Probably fraudulent,' said Lucy with a grimace.

'Probably. At any rate, she was attracted to him and he to her – or to her money – and they became lovers.'

'Was this before or after Brinton had become involved with Campbell?' someone asked.

'That involvement goes way back to Scotland. You'll remember Nigel is pretty certain Brinton was Campbell's "shadowy figure", but Campbell was very much in the background at the point when Brinton and Marilyn became a couple.' That was Alan's contribution. 'The Met, and our people, and Nigel here, have been burning up cyberspace tracking down all the connections. They've also learned what the connection was with Crane. He invested some money with Brinton, and of course lost it because of Brinton's fraud. The trouble was it wasn't his money. He'd borrowed it from the Apsley House Foundation, intending to make a lot of money for them. The Brintons found out about it and were able to blackmail him into lending his car. They did not, of course, explain to him exactly how they planned to use it.' Alan took a very large swallow of his ale.

I continued. 'So to shorten a very long story, Marilyn became pregnant, inherited a gazillion dollars, to use Lucy's term, and married Robert. He continued to pile up money through illegal stock deals and eventually joined Campbell in the lucrative fake-charity scheme.

'The fly in the ointment was that the SEC was becoming more and more interested in these activities, and Marilyn was becoming less and less interested in Robert. So she came up with a brilliant idea. No mean plotter, is our Marilyn. She had never met Campbell, but from a few things Robert had said, she had deduced that Iain was either homosexual or asexual. So she proposed that Robert "marry" Iain. The two could then make identical wills leaving everything to the other.'

'And then Iain would have a convenient accident, and the Brintons would be even richer.' Fred shook his head in disgust.

'But would the wills be valid?' the dean objected. 'Since the marriage wasn't, I mean.'

'We've seen a copy,' said Alan. 'The Met has, I mean. Neither uses the word "spouse" referring to the legatee, just the word "partner", which, I'm told, has no legal meaning.'

'But what about the law that won't let you cut your spouse out?' Lucy asked. 'Wouldn't that make Brinton's will invalid?'

'Perhaps. The laws vary from state to state, and I don't know what the Illinois statutes require. In any case, it didn't matter. Once Campbell was dead, Brinton's will was null and void anyway.'

'So Marilyn arranged for Campbell's death through her friend Mr Respectable.'

'Crane, my dear,' Alan put in.

'I know, but I like Mr Respectable better. And I suppose they'll never find the guy who did the actual driving. Anyway, Iain died. Marilyn had sent Robert over to this side of the pond, ostensibly to make sure everything worked out properly. As a bonus, she was going to plant some evidence that would lead the police to Robert as the murderer, which would get him nicely out of her way, too.'

'But things didn't go as planned!' Lucy was grimly jubilant. 'Thanks to you, Uncle Alan. And Aunt Dorothy. You two wouldn't leave it alone, and in the end Robert became a liability to Marilyn. He figured that out and started hiding from her, just in case. *And* he decided to get rid of me, hoping that would confuse matters enough that he could get away to someplace that doesn't have an extradition treaty with the UK *or* the US. But it didn't work, thanks to our heroic little Mike!'

Mike, hearing his name, thought it might be safe to venture out. Maybe all those noisy people had gone home. He came to the kitchen door, peered out, and vanished again.

'Our brave hero!' said someone, to a gale of laughter.

* * *

'What's going to happen to them?' asked Lucy when all our guests had left. Mike had reappeared and demanded food, and was now curled up in Lucy's lap, Watson at her feet.

'The Brintons? Heaven knows,' said Alan with a yawn. 'There are so many different jurisdictions involved in different countries, they may well die of old age before it's all settled. They'll probably be much poorer by the time the SEC get done with them, if they're required to repay the victims of the various frauds.'

'I have a hard time feeling sorry for them!' I said tartly. 'I do worry about their children, though. Speaking of victims.'

'I'll look into that when I get back to Chicago,' said Lucy. 'They'll be all right. Probably better, to be out of that toxic home.'

'So you're certainly going back?' I said. 'We had hoped . . .'

'I have obligations, Aunt Lucy. Parkwood is reluctant to let me go. And of course I haven't seen my poor kitty in ages. But I'll be back. Soon, I hope.'

'Back to stay?'

'I'm thinking about it. I can do my work anywhere there's a computer. And one of the reasons I was so happy with this speaking gig at the university was that I've been wanting to re-discover my English roots. I've realized, staying here, that my heart is really English, no matter how Americanized I've become. I do have to decide what to do about Fred, if he's really interested in me, but I can't bear the thought of losing touch with you. You're really my only family!' She brushed back a tear. We pretended not to see.

Alan cleared his throat. 'That brings me to a point. Dorothy and I have discussed the possibility, hinging on your approval, of course, that is—'

'What Alan is trying to say,' I broke in, speaking through tears of my own, 'is that we'd like to adopt you. Formally, I mean. You really are family, and we'd like to make it official. If you'd like it, I mean.'

She stood up, greatly to the displeasure of Mike, who stalked off. We joined in a teary, messy group hug, all the animals intertwined. 'Mum, Dad – I can't think of anything I'd like more. Look at the family I'll be joining!'

Emmy and Sam uttered non-committal sounds. Watson barked happily. Mike jumped to Lucy's shoulder and patted her cheek.

Jane, who had entered without our noticing, had the final word. 'Thought so,' she said in her gruff voice. But tears were running down her cheeks, too.

AUTHOR'S NOTE

This book would not have happened without the help of my friend, Elizabeth Duncan. She and I met at a conference years ago and decided it would be fun if we wrote each other's characters into our books. So Penny Brannigan has visited Dorothy and Alan on several occasions, and Dorothy and Alan have made a few trips to Wales to see Penny. Elizabeth and I were exchanging emails about how hard it was to come up with good plots when she suggested an outline for what became this book. Then Penny and her new husband Colin walked into the book with a few more twists. Elizabeth, here's to you!

I also owe profound thanks to Jaime Owen, who has been my first reader for several books now, and has offered valuable suggestions.

The reader should know that the book is set at some future time when the COVID pandemic has receded and travel is again possible. As I write this, that relief seems almost in sight. I very much hope that by the time you read *A Deadly Web*, the pandemic will be only a nasty memory.

Ingram Content Group UK Ltd.
Milton Keynes UK
UKHW020155040523
421181UK00006B/398